"I've never been kissed like that"

Francesca confessed honestly, and then asked, "If you wanted to kiss me, why are you hurrying away instead of doing it again?" Shyly she placed her hands on his chest, her face raised to his.

For an instant she thought he was going to repeat his earlier embrace, then he pushed her away. "Because kissing you was a mistake," he said dryly. "You think you're in love, but it may be only an infatuation."

Francesca wanted to protest, *it's not, it's not.* But Caspar went on, "You've seen too little as yet to know where your future lies. And what happened last night doesn't change anything. It was only a kiss, for heaven's sake!"

Only a kiss. Only the most magical, world-changing experience of her life....

ANNE WEALE
is also the author of these

Harlequin Romances

and these

Harlequin Presents

Many of these titles are available at your local bookseller.

For a free catalogue listing all available Harlequin Romances and Harlequin Presents, send your name and address to:

HARLEQUIN READER SERVICE
1440 South Priest Drive, Tempe, AZ 85281
Canadian address: Stratford, Ontario N5A 6W2

Rain of
Diamonds

by

ANNE WEALE

Harlequin Books

TORONTO • LONDON • LOS ANGELES • AMSTERDAM
SYDNEY • HAMBURG • PARIS • STOCKHOLM • ATHENS • TOKYO

Original hardcover edition published in 1981
by Mills & Boon Limited

ISBN 0-373-02436-3

Harlequin edition published October 1981

CHAPTER ONE

FRANCESCA was at her drawing-board, but her pencil was twirling idly between her slim fingers—chunky silver rings on her left hand, coils of Indian gold on her right—when the chirping note of the house-telephone disturbed her frowning abstractedness.

She reached for the receiver. 'Yes?'

'The Countess is arriving,' said the voice of her show-room assistant.

The Countess had been one of Francesca's first important customers when she opened her shop in the short street called Beauchamp Place where many of the most fashionable women in London—and indeed from all parts of the world—came in search of elegant clothes and amusing accessories.

'I'll come down at once. Thank you, Susie.'

Francesca slid off her stool and glanced briefly out of the window from which she could see the roof of a beige Rolls-Royce, and a woman in furs stepping out of it.

The chauffeur who, elsewhere, would have opened the door for her, was still at the wheel, waiting to move on as soon as possible. Eighty years earlier, other vehicles would have had to wait while a countess descended from her carriage. But in those days the narrow terraced houses in Beauchamp Place, each with its short flight of steps, had been private homes, not boutiques.

In modern London, even a countess could not aggravate the perpetual traffic jam in a street not designed to accommodate a constant procession of delivery vans, taxis, and the cars of drivers making a detour to avoid the even greater congestion where Brompton Road merged with Knightsbridge.

At the time of the Countess's arrival, Francesca was in the second-floor studio-cum-stockroom which was where she created the beautiful, distinctive evening clothes which, in three years, had made the name Franca da Rimini almost as well known as that of Zandra Rhodes and Gina Fratini.

One influential fashion magazine had even compared her with Mary McFadden, the American designer. But Francesca knew that it was her financial backing as much as her talent which had saved her the long hard climb to achieve recognition. Without that backing it might have been ten years or more before she could have set up in business anywhere, let alone in a part of London where her designs could not fail to catch the eye of the type of customer on whom her success depended.

Before going down to the showroom, she checked her appearance in the full-length mirror near the door. There were days, and this had turned out to be one of them, when she saw her reflection as if it were that of a stranger. This is not me, Francesca Hartley, she would think, looking at the image of herself in the looking-glass.

What happened to me?—to the girl I used to be? The original Francesca.

Possibly this was an experience shared by thousands of people besides herself. She could not be the only woman who had, hidden within her, another and quite different person from the one whom the world saw.

Perhaps it was the nature of all human beings to suffer a metamorphosis from the person they had dreamed of becoming to the person shaped by events over which they had no control. Perhaps *he* was equally changed.

At this thought, the mental discipline which, like the perfect physical control of a ballet dancer, she had learned by long and hard practice, helped her to close her mind to the past and return to the present.

'Good afternoon, Lady Cornwall,' she said, as she entered the showroom and found the young, fox-furred

Countess in conversation with her assistant.

'Hello, Franca. How are you? I can't wait to see this new dress Susie told me about while you were in Italy.'

The Countess herself had recently returned from a winter holiday in Fiji. Her face, under a large red fox hat to match the top-quality 'cherry' skins of her coat, was as brown as Francesca's had once been, a long time ago.

'I hope you'll like it,' said Francesca, allowing a slight note of doubt to enter her voice because she was perfectly certain the Countess would find it irresistible.

Lady Cornwall tugged off her hat and, with Susie's help, shed her coat, revealing a slender figure in a sweater of palest grey cashmere, with trousers of the same colour tucked into pale grey suede boots.

She sat down on the Sheraton sofa which was hidden from passers-by by a screen of black and gold lacquer which formed a partial backdrop to the window display.

The rest of the showroom was open to view from the street, and window-shoppers could see the rails of dresses in the fitments all around the walls; dresses of satin and velvet, dresses of rustling silk taffeta and misty silk gauze, dresses which all bore the invisible signature *Franca da Rimini*, which was what made the women who wore them feel a favoured élite.

Second-hand, they were snatched off the racks of the high-class dress agencies within a short time of being hung there. They had an undating quality which made them wearable for season after season. In general they were discarded only by the very richest women, such as the Countess, who could afford to buy several each year.

Francesca did not show a collection as such. She went on designing all year round, earlier styles being discontinued as new ones were added. Always there were about fifty dresses or combinations of separates on show, but sometimes a very special design was not made public immediately. It was kept out of sight in a cupboard, to be shown to particular patrons whose custom deserved special treatment. One of these was a Royal Princess, another an Italian film star. A third was the Countess.

In Francesca's absence in Italy, she had come to the shop in search of something to wear at the first important social function of the London season. This, though neither as formal nor exclusive as it had once been, still took place every year, beginning with the Berkeley Dress Show, the models being girls who were 'coming out', and the Rose Ball at Grosvenor House, and ending with Cowes Week.

Susie, knowing that the Princess was pregnant and the actress on long location, had confided to the Countess that today there was a new design due in from the workroom. As Lady Cornwall settled herself expectantly on the sofa, Susie went to the mirror-fronted cupboard in which the dress was awaiting its private view.

Francesca, although she knew what to expect, and had herself worked the prototype for its embroideries, had not yet seen the finished dress.

She had not returned from Italy until late the previous night and it had not arrived when she left the shop for a luncheon engagement. When she returned and Susie told her it had come, she had answered, with a lack of interest which had caused her assistant much puzzlement, 'I'll look at it later, when Lady Cornwall comes, Susie.'

The reason for her uncharacteristic indifference had been that the man who had asked her to lunch with him at Ma Cuisine, round the corner in Walton Street, had also asked her to marry him.

She had refused his proposal and, in so doing, ended a friendship which she knew she would miss; as perhaps she might come to regret rejecting a closer relationship.

This was why she had been lost in thought when the telephone rang in the studio a few minutes earlier.

Susie brought the dress out with a flourish, making the skirt swirl and shimmer. It was dark blue. Or was it green? The colour changed with every movement, a mys-

terious effect achieved only after long experiment with
layers of different coloured tulles between a top layer of
chiffon and an under-layer of shot silk. Stitched to the
tulles in between were silver sequins, green beads, shining
glass bugles and brilliants.

It was by far the most ambitious and costly idea that
Francesca had ever translated into reality. It made Lady
Cornwall jump up and, seizing the hanger from Susie,
hold the dress against herself.

'It's stunning, Franca . . . simply gorgeous! You've
really excelled yourself with this.'

'I'm glad you like it.'

'I adore it. I can't wait to wear it.'

'It's rather expensive, I'm afraid. All that complicated
embroidery . . .'

'I don't care what it costs,' said the Countess, with the
airy unconcern of a woman married to someone who,
unlike the majority of aristocrats, was still a man of vast
wealth. 'May I try it on? Is it my size?'

Francesca nodded. The dress had been made a size
twelve—Lady Cornwall's size, and her own.

With Susie to assist her with the fastenings, the Countess disappeared into the fitting-room.

Francesca turned her green gaze on the busy street. It
was spring, a time of the year that always made her feel
restless. Born in England, but long exiled from it, she had
come back in the spring of the year. But a country spring
among lanes white with Queen Anne's Lace, and hedges
foaming with lilac.

Now her career confined her to London, which she
found enormously stimulating. Less than half a mile from
the shop was that great treasure house of applied arts, the
Victoria and Albert Museum, the source of much inspiration to her. Equally nearby was Harrods, with its super-
lative Food Halls, and not far away were Hyde Park and
Kensington Gardens where she could walk on grass, or sit
on a bench watching the ducks on the Serpentine or the

model boats on the Round Pond.

In many ways she agreed with the great Doctor Samuel Johnson's dictum: *When a man is tired of London he is tired of life; for there is in London all that life can afford.*

Not quite all, she thought, with a sigh. Not golden warmth all year round. Not the creak of a helm, or the sudden rattle of a winch. Not the sun rising out of the sea, or the momentary green flash at sunset, followed by nightfall and starlight.

'What mystifies me,' said the Countess, as she reappeared, 'is where you get your ideas. This dress is different from anything you've done before.'

She postured in front of the mirror, twisting and turning to inspect her reflection from every angle.

Francesca said, 'The idea for this dress came to me when I remembered leaning over the bows of a boat on a night when the sea was phosphorescent. Every so often a shoal of flying fish would flash through the water like shooting stars.'

'When was that? On a cruise?' asked her client.

'Of a sort—yes.'

Francesca saw that the dress needed one or two slight adjustments to make it a faultless fit. As she measured and noted the alterations, on impulse, she asked, 'Do your family jewels include such a thing as a rain of diamonds, Lady Cornwall?'

'I don't think so. Why do you ask?'

'It's the perfect jewel for this dress.'

'I'm not even sure what it is. A rain of diamonds, you say?'

'Yes. I've never seen one myself, but I had it described to me once, and I had it in mind when I was designing this. An original rain of diamonds is early Victorian, and perhaps rather rare nowadays.'

'I know my husband's mother had a great many of his grandmother's jewels re-set in the style of the Twenties because Victorian settings were considered old-fashioned and hideous. Now, of course, I'm beginning to wish that I hadn't had most of *her* clips and bracelets re-set, because they're coming back into fashion,' said the Countess.

After a pause, she went on, 'Perhaps I could find a rain of diamonds. Sotheby's may have sold one recently, or Harvey & Gore may have one. I'll make enquiries. Now about shoes? What do you think?'

Francesca made several suggestions, and eventually it was agreed that she would liaise with another shop in Beauchamp Place which specialised in bespoke shoes and boots, and would make up evening slippers designed especially for the dress and embellished with similar em-broidery.

When, after the Countess had gone, and Susie would have packed the dress in a box to go back to the work-room, Francesca took it from her and held it against her-self.

'It would suit you better than it does Lady Cornwall,' remarked her assistant. 'She's rather too fair for it, I think. It's a dress for your lovely colouring.'

Francesca's hair was a rich brown with reddish tints, and her eyebrows and lashes were darker.

'I designed it for myself,' she admitted. 'But as an ex-ercise only, not actually to wear it. I never go to any functions that call for a dress of this sort.'

She detected in Susie's expression the incomprehension of a girl who, given her employer's opportunities, would have courted rather than avoided the social life and pub-licity enjoyed by most successful designers. But Francesca had reasons for shunning all personal publicity, even under her professional pseudonym. Very few people—not all her friends—knew that Franca was not her real name but a contraction of it; or that, although she did have foreign blood in her, the surname da Rimini had nothing to do with her Italian forebears.

She had chosen it out of a fellow-feeling for another

Francesca who, in Ravenna nearly seven hundred years earlier, with Paolo, the handsome younger brother of the unpleasant man her parents had forced her to marry, had been put to death for their adultery.

Not that Francesca herself had ever been guilty of that offence; but she knew that, in the same circumstances, if the man she had loved had wanted her, she would have risked any punishment to have spent one night in his arms.

'I must get back to work,' she said briskly, handing the dress back to Susie.

As she passed through the arch at the back of the shop to the staircase, someone opened the door of the draught-lobby inside the street door.

Francesca glanced over her shoulder, knowing that whoever had entered would be visible in the gilt mirror on the far side of the showroom.

It was not a woman but a man who had caused the door-bell to purr. A very tall man with black hair, and a face as sun-tanned as Lady Cornwall's.

Speaking to Susie, he said, 'Good afternoon. I was expecting to find a friend here.'   At the sound of his voice, Francesca's green eyes dilated, and she gave a stifled gasp. She had thought her eyes must have deceived her; that it could not be him, merely someone extraordinarily like him.

But the voice—deep and slightly drawling when it was not crisp and incisive—she could never mistake, though it was so long since the last time she had heard it.

'There is no one here at the moment, but you're welcome to wait, sir,' said Susie.

'May I? Thank you, I will,' was his answer.

'Won't you sit down?'

Without being able to see her, Francesca could visualise her assistant's gesture towards the sofa.

His reflection disappeared from the mirror, and instinctively Francesca drew back into an area of gloom at the foot of the flight. She saw him sit down on the sofa, and her heart began to beat so violently that she put both hands to her chest as if to muffle a sound which might otherwise draw his attention.

How little, compared with herself, he had changed since the last time she saw him. Perhaps the long grooves down his cheeks were fractionally deeper than they had been. But his body was still lean and limber, his jawline still clear-cut and forceful.

She heard Susie ask, 'You're quite sure this is the right shop?'

'I'm certain it is. You may not know her by name, but my friend gave me the impression of being one of your most enthusiastic customers,' the man replied with a smile.

Time had not diminished his magnetism, nor his interest in the opposite sex, Francesca observed. Susie was an attractive young woman, and his smile acknowledged the fact.

'I take it you're not the owner of this establishment?' he went on.

'Oh, no—I just work here,' said Susie.

'Is there really a Signora or Signorina da Rimini, or is that just a name on the fascia?' he asked, in the tone of a man making any conversation which occurred to him with a girl pleasing to his eye.

But although she could always be relied on to make herself pleasant to the husbands and men friends of customers, Susie drew the line at flirting with any of them. Personable as he was, in her eyes the tall man was not to be compared with the equally tall young police officer who had placed the modest engagement ring on her left hand, and whom she was planning to marry before the end of the year.

Had the man on the sofa been unknown to her, Francesca would have been amused by the faint note of reproof with which her assistant replied, 'Everything you

see here was designed by Miss da Rimini, sir. She's upstairs in her studio now.'

'Ah, but is she the glamorous creature such a name
suggests?' was his comeback. 'Or is she perhaps a stout
party on the wrong side of fifty, born in Aldgate?'

Clearly he knew that many of the fashions sold in the
West End of London had their origins in the East End
where some of them could be bought for a fraction of the
boutique prices by those in the know.

Francesca drew a deep breath and walked forward to
stand in the archway.

'Perhaps you should judge for yourself,' she said, in her
low but clear voice.

Very slowly he rose to his feet, the bantering gleam in
his eyes replaced by a stare of incredulity.

'*Francesca!*'

'You were right: there is no such person as Franca da
Rimini. But my own name isn't as glamorous, and I
had . . . other reasons for wanting to keep it to myself.'

Her self-possession amazed her. Now that the first
shock of seeing him again had worn off, she felt astonish-
ingly collected.

'What an unlikely place for us to meet again after all
this time,' she said lightly.

'No more unlikely than where we met for the first
time.'

After the curious huskiness with which he had uttered
her real name, now his tone matched hers in its coolness.

But his eyes were not cool. They were blazing with
fierce, savage anger.

And as, with Susie a perplexed onlooker, they stood
silently gazing at each other, Francesca had the illusion
that the years between had evaporated, and she was her
real self again, in that faraway place which she had never
forgotten, on a day she would remember until she
died . . .

CHAPTER TWO

'Hey!—You, boy! Come over here!'

Roused from her somnolent daydreams by the brisk, authoritative voice, Francesca stirred and looked round her to see by whom and to whom the words had been spoken.

The wharf, at that hour, was deserted. Between noon and mid-afternoon the heat of the sun was intense, the humidity killing. Most people slept through those hours.

Sometimes Francesca slept too. But the night before Andrew, her father, had drunk late and deep at the *cantina*. He was still sleeping it off and as, because money was short, they were sharing the cheapest room in the town's one seedy hotel, the sound and the sour-wine fumes of his stertorous breathing had driven her out on to the quay which formed one side of the *plaza*.

Earlier, while hanging out the much-mended blue cotton shirt which, with the one she was wearing, two pairs of equally shabby jeans and one pair of cheap *alpargatas*, formed her entire wardrobe, she had noticed a new arrival among the half dozen vessels berthed at the quayside. But at that time there had been no signs of life on board the forty-foot sloop which had put in there during the night.

Now a man was standing on deck. As she looked at him, he beckoned her with a gesture as commanding as his tone of voice.

In her short, footloose, unsheltered life, Francesca had met a great many different kinds of men, and learnt not to trust any of them; not even her father, on whom she could never depend not to waste all the money he earned on one of his periodic binges.

The man who had summoned her to him was not easy to place in any of the categories familiar to her. He had the height and the broad-shouldered build of a *gringo*, a term used in South America to refer to a person from North America, or one with fair hair, or indeed any species of foreigner.

It was difficult to be certain on the strength of a few words addressed to her while she was drowsy, but she thought Spanish was not his mother tongue. Nor was it hers, but, having learnt it as a child, she could pass for a *mestizo* or half-breed. Many people took her to be Andrew's natural son by an Indian woman because, although Francesca had green eyes and hair which, when clean, had the rich brown sheen of mahogany, there was something about her cheekbones and the slight upward slant of her eyes that hinted at Indian blood in her. In fact her mother had been an Italian from whom Francesca took her name, but of whom she had no recollection.

Certainly as she slid off the stack of bales and advanced in the direction of the stranger, there was nothing to suggest that, on her mother's side, she was the legitimate descendant of one of Italy's oldest families.

'What do you want?' she enquired, keeping her voice as gruff as possible.

Fortunately, hers was by nature a low-pitched voice, while most of the half-grown local youths had voices a tone or two lighter than those of their *gringo* counterparts. So far, no one had detected that the tousle-haired son of the artist was, in fact, not his son but his daughter.

How much longer she and her father could continue to practise this deception depended on how much longer her body remained thin and coltish. Perhaps because, for several years, they had lived on an inadequate diet, she had come to womanhood later than was usual among the early-flowering Latin girls in the countries through which they had roamed their nomadic way. And even now, at an age when a true *mestizo* would have had at least a couple of babies clinging to her skirts, Francesca's breasts were still small enough to be unnoticeable under a baggy shirt, and her hips were boyishly narrow.

As she drew near the sloop, the man flipped a coin in the air and caught it in a lean brown hand.

'Would you like to earn this, boy?'

'Doing what, *señor?*'

Long familiar with the seamy side of life, Francesca knew that although her disguise protected her from many men, it didn't make her safe from them all.

More than once, when touting one of her father's paintings round the café tables in a big city, she had felt a hand on her backside and whipped round to find someone leering at her with a meaning smirk which had changed to an ugly scowl when she had expressed her disgust with a pithy phrase learnt from the other gutter-snipes.

Not that this man looked like a *maricón*, but it paid to be wary of everyone until you knew something about them.

He said, 'I've lost my crew and I need someone to run a few errands for me. Not immediately. Later on, when the place opens up.' His hard grey eyes turned from her to scrutinise the rundown waterfront. 'If I go ashore myself, I may come back to find I've also lost half my rigging.'

'Yes, there are many thieves here,' Francesca agreed.

'Including you, I shouldn't wonder,' the man murmured, eyeing her sardonically.

He had spoken in English, and she surprised him by retorting, 'No, I do not steal—or not yet.'

He tilted a well-shaped dark eyebrow as black as his hair. 'Not yet?'

She shrugged. 'When people who have almost nothing see others with more than they need, naturally they're tempted to redress the balance a little. I might steal if I were hungry. Perhaps you might also, *señor*.'

Even as she said this she regretted letting him know that she could speak his language, and thereby arousing his curiosity.

Had she but known it, her fluent command of English was made all the more extraordinary by the fact that she spoke it with a patrician accent totally at variance with her uncultured Spanish, and her down-at-heel, scruffy appearance. However, as she had never mixed with her compatriots, or indeed with any other *gringos* except those of the most dubious type, she had no idea that her English was in any way unusual.

'Perhaps I might,' he agreed. 'You don't look well fed, I must say. Shall I find you something to eat?'

She reverted to Spanish. 'If you can spare it, *señor*.'

The man said, still in his own tongue, 'You can come aboard, but I don't want you coming below. I have enough problems at the moment without having to fumigate and, as well as a month on square meals, you look as if you could do with a good hosing down, boy.'

As he disappeared between decks, she saw that his bare suntanned back was as powerfully muscled as his chest.

His brown skin glistened with the sweat induced by the humidity, and renewed her envy of men's freedom to go about stripped to the waist.

Often she longed to go naked, or to wear shorts instead of long pants. But Andrew said that her legs, with their rounded knees and slender ankles, were unmistakably a girl's legs.

Although the Englishman had implied that she might be verminous, and it was a miracle that she wasn't, somehow she avoided the many unpleasant contagions of downtown life in the tropics.

Prickly heat was the worst she had suffered, because every night, while her father was propping up bars, she would wash herself from head to foot. She would have liked to wash her hair more frequently, but in a place where lank, unwashed hair was the norm, she dared not keep it clean and shining. She would comb it at night, but not in the morning; and although she detested the broken, black state of her nails, it was better than attracting attention. In most of the places they visited, poor women were childbearing chattels, or *putas* in frowsty bordels. Francesca had no illusions about what might happen to her if someone detected her sex and chose to assault her on a night when Andrew was in no condition to protect her.

Not that he was much protection when he was sober, for he was not a tall, strong man like the one who had just gone below to fetch her some food. Andrew Hartley's most strenuous exercise was raising his elbow and, less and less frequently nowadays, putting a paintbrush to canvas.

The Englishman came back on deck, carrying in one hand a sandwich and in the other a can of beer. As he handed the thick sandwich to her, Francesca noticed that his nails were neatly pared and as clean as seashells. It made her ashamed of her own; and, for the first time, resentful. If Andrew would save enough money to pay their fare to some more civilised place, she could grow her nails like other girls, and file the tips smooth, and buff them.

Then her first big bite of the sandwich, which consisted of a length of crusty bread split and filled with meat and tomato, made her forget everything but this unforeseen feast.

Her thin cheeks bulging as she munched, she watched him strip off the tab which sealed the can. Instead of dropping it on the deck, or tossing it over the side, as most people she knew would have done, he put it in the pocket of his shorts.

Unlike the short, bowed, hairless legs of the South American Indians, and the usually thickly furred legs of the men of Spanish descent, his long legs were not very hairy, and his chest and shoulders were smooth, although he had a strong beard which even at this hour of day showed as a dark shadow upon his lean cheeks and square jaw.

'What are you doing here?' he asked her. 'You surely weren't born in this place?'

Francesca's mouth was still full, and she could not answer immediately. She was capable, when it seemed prudent, of assuming the uncouth manners of the people among whom she lived. Along with her father, she copied his way of eating. Now, although she was still not sure he was entirely to be trusted, somehow she felt it was unnecessary to play the pig for the Englishman.

'No, we're just passing through,' she said, still sticking to Spanish.

An idea was forming in her mind. Perhaps, as he had lost his crew, he might take them aboard as working passengers. It didn't much matter where he meant to go next. Anywhere would be an improvement on this place.

'Who are "we"?' he enquired.

'My father and I.'

The man drank some beer. 'What's your name?'

She answered without hesitation, 'Paco, *señor*.'

It was an affectionate diminutive for Spanish boys named Francisco after the saint who began life as the indulged son of a rich merchant and died the founder of a famous order of poor friars. As her real name was first borne by St Francesca of Rome, named after St Francis of Assisi, the nickname Paco had seemed an appropriate choice to foster the impression that she was her father's half-breed son.

'My father is English . . . an artist . . . and a very good one,' she added, more truthfully.

'And your mother?'

She shrugged. 'She died long ago. I don't remember her, *señor*.'

'Your father may have a great talent, but he doesn't

appear to be too successful on a commercial plane, judging by the way he feeds and clothes you,' was his next remark.

Her firm, rather stubborn chin lifted. 'Sometimes the most brilliant artists are not recognised during their lifetime; and the places where my father paints his best pictures are not ones where it is easy to sell a painting. Who, here, could afford such a thing?'

'Perhaps I might, if I shared your opinion of his talent. What's your father's name?'

'Andrew Hartley. And your name, *señor*?'

'Barrington. Caspar Barrington.'

'Perhaps when I've finished your errands, you would like me to bring you two or three paintings to look at?'

'Why can't I see them at your place? Where do you live? Here in town?'

'Outside the town there is only the forest,' she answered. 'We're staying at the hotel over there. But the light isn't good in our room. You need good light to look at paintings.'

'Very well. Ask your father to meet me in the hotel bar at six o'clock. Perhaps, if we take to each other, I may invite him to supper.'

'And me, too?' she couldn't help asking.

A slight smile touched his firm mouth. 'Still hungry, are you? We'll see. Perhaps, and again perhaps not. It does seem, on closer inspection, that you're not quite as scruffy an urchin as you seemed to be at first glance.'

As he spoke he took hold of her ear and, none too gently, inspected it.

'A clean ear. Strange!' was his comment. 'At your age most boys have ears like mushroom beds. How old are you? Fourteen? Fifteen?'

She guessed he was judging her age by the absence of down round her lips, and the somewhat girlish appearance which some boys had at the stage before their shoulders grew wider and their arm and wrist muscles thickened.

Ignoring the question, she said, 'My father is a very clean man. You mustn't judge him by me, sir. He's like you—*es todo un señor*'—using the Spanish expression meaning 'He's a real gentleman.'

It was an unconscious lapse into the smarmy respect of street arabs flattering and fawning prospective customers, and often, with those newly rich, it could prove extremely effective.

But Caspar Barrington's reaction was to cuff her sufficiently hard to make her eyes water.

'You know nothing about me, my lad, so cut out that unctuous rubbish if you don't want to have both your ears boxed. And speak English, please. Can you read?'

Francesca nodded, blinking back tears of indignation at his roughness, and yet knowing she had invited it by treating him like one of the upstarts to be seen in the cafés of the cities, with loud suits to match their loud voices, and gold teeth and many gold rings, and above all a fine contempt for all those they thought their inferiors. This man was not one of those, and she saw she would have to be careful not to annoy him a second time or it might ruin her hope of escape.

'Read that,' he instructed, giving her a list of the four or five things he needed to replenish his stores.

His writing was clear and well formed; the hand of a man of education. She read out the list, and he nodded and gave her some money.

'And don't think you needn't come back, because if you don't reappear, I shall find you, and take my belt to you,' he warned, touching the Mexican silver buckle which clasped the plaited leather belt which was passed through the loops of his shorts.

Her green eyes flashed with annoyance. 'I've told you—I'm not a thief!'

'I hope not—for your sake. Off you go.' He drained his beer, and went below.

Before she dealt with his list, Francesca raced back to their room to talk to her father. She found him awake, but nursing a hangover headache.

'For God's sake, girl! Must you burst in like that?' he complained, his hands to his scalp.

He was not yet fifty years old, but he looked like a man nearing sixty.

Knowing it was useless to talk to him until she had ministered to his headache, Francesca gave him some aspirins and a diluted measure of a spirit purporting to be brandy.

When he seemed to be capable of attending, she said, 'Father, you must listen. I've been talking to another Englishman. He may buy one of your paintings, and he *may*—if we play our cards right—give us a lift down the river. He wants you to meet him downstairs in the bar at six o'clock. So please, whatever you feel like, do try to brace up and be nice. You've nearly two hours to recover. It's our one chance, Father—our one chance.'

The desperate note in her voice seemed to penetrate his self-absorption. He peered at her, haggard and red-eyed, a wreck of the good-looking man she remembered from earlier years.

'What do you mean—our one chance? We can leave any time we feel like it.'

'Oh, Father, you know we can't. Not without money, and you always spend all our money on drink and playing cards.'

'Don't nag. You don't do so badly. We may be a bit up against it for the time being, but it's only a temporary setback. We've had our good times, remember. There are men who, in my position, would have left you behind in an orphanage. How would you have liked that, my girl?'

This was always his answer to reproaches, and she knew it was probably true: most men would have dumped her somewhere. Why Andrew had chosen to keep her was a mystery she could never fathom. Perhaps, in those days, he had still had some sense of responsibility.

It was equally true that her life with him had not been all bad. He had always drunk, but he had not always been a drunkard, and some of the women who had taken up with him after her mother's death had been pretty and merry, and kind to the little Francesca.

It was only during her teens that he had gone steadily downhill, slowly destroying all her natural affection and becoming a burden too heavy for her youthful shoulders.

'If you want to stay . . . stay,' she retorted, with sudden impatience. 'But I want to leave with Mr Barrington. I must leave here, Father—I must! I can't go on living like this . . . always worried . . . always afraid.'

'Oh, very well,' Andrew said irritably. 'I'll come down and talk to this fellow, and ask him to give us a passage as far as the coast. What's he doing here up-river? Trading?'

'I don't know. I shouldn't think so. I have to go out now—he's asked me to buy some stores for him. I shan't be more than half an hour, then I'll come back and help you to get ready.'

Getting him ready began with giving him a shave with an old-fashioned cut-throat razor which his own hands were far too unsteady to wield, but which she had learned to use as skilfully as any barber.

The paucity of her wardrobe was not matched by his. His tropical suits and silk shirts might have seen better days, but Francesca had always been quick to deal with stains and repairs so that, on occasion, Andrew could still present quite a dapper appearance to the world.

Caspar Barrington was already seated at a table in the bar-cum-dining-room when they went downstairs. He had chosen one close to the window through which he could keep an eye on the sloop.

As he rose to shake hands with her father, Francesca sent up a prayer that the two men would take to each other.

She had brought down a couple of boards, one a portrait of an old woman, and one a view of the river. But she propped them against her chair and did not refer to them until he himself asked to see them.

As he studied them, his expression gave nothing away, and she wondered how much he knew about good and bad paintings, and whether her father's work was not really as good as she had always supposed it to be.

At length, addressing himself to Andrew, he said, 'How much are you asking for these?'

'A song, my dear fellow, a song.' Andrew named a price far higher than she would have asked.

'In a show at Colnaghi's, perhaps they might fetch that,' was the younger man's dry rejoinder. 'But this isn't Bond Street, Hartley. I'll give you one third of your asking price. Take it or leave it.'

Andrew opened his mouth to argue, but Francesca intervened swiftly, 'You're getting a bargain, Mr Barrington, but we can't afford to refuse your offer.'

'If you'll bring them aboard, I'll pay you there. I never flash money around in places like this,' he said, looking over her head at the shifty-eyed barman.

They followed him on board the sloop. When she saw the comfortable saloon with its wood-panelled bulkheads, tobacco linen squabs and curtains, and laminated plastic dining table, she could not contain an exclamation of pleasure.

It all looked so clean and shipshape; so different from their present quarters with the mildewed walls, and the rickety balcony shaded by a broken *persiana* with the paint peeling off its slats.

In a very short time the table was set for a meal which their host described as pot-luck, but which seemed to Francesca a banquet. It was years since she had eaten so well, and she found it astonishing that the rich chicken and vegetable stew, accompanied by a bowl of rice, had been prepared by a man. Andrew knew nothing of such arts and nor, to her secret dismay, did he do the meal justice. She had to eat most of his for him, hurriedly changing over their plates when Caspar Barrington went to the galley for a second bottle of wine, and hoping he wouldn't notice that her father had eaten only two or three mouthfuls.

Although there were no awkward pauses in the men's conversation, she would have been blind not to see the sceptical gleam in Caspar Barrington's eyes when her father was describing their travels in a way which bore little resemblance to the squalid truth.

Towards the end of the meal, she began to nudge Andrew's foot to remind him to bring up the subject of working a passage to the seaport which lay a hundred miles downstream. But he chose to ignore her signals, and just as she was deciding to broach the matter herself, Caspar Barrington paid him for the paintings. Whereupon, to her horror, Andrew proposed a game of cards.

'Oh, no Father—no!' she protested.

'By all means,' Caspar Barrington said smoothly. He glanced at her anxious face. 'Go to bed, Paco, if you're tired.'

'No, I'm not tired,' she muttered.

As he took a clean pack of cards from one of the lockers, she had a sinking premonition that before very long the notes which her father had pocketed would be restored to the sloop's enigmatic skipper.

Although her father had made a number of oblique enquiries about what had brought him up-river, and how he made his living, they still knew little about him. Perhaps he was a professional gambler, in which case Andrew wouldn't stand a chance, for although he was not a poor player, luck was never with him. He seemed always to be on a losing streak.

However, when her father suggested the stakes they should play for, the other man surprised her by replying, 'I don't play for money, Hartley. I'm surprised that you do—with strangers. This continent has more than its share of vicious characters, and I've seen more than one nasty fracas sparked off by a quarrel at cards.'

He shuffled the pack with the same deft precision with which he had laid and cleared the table. The steadiness of his strong, shapely hands made the tremor of her father's the more noticeable. She wondered how old Caspar Barrington was, and found it difficult to judge. He had a young man's lithe movements, and his black hair was thick and springy, yet the tanned face was that of a man who had seen a great deal of the world and was marked by deep lines down his cheeks and many small lines round his eyes.

He could not be said to be handsome in the way that her father had once been, but he looked shrewd and tough and virile; and it had not escaped her notice that, while they were crossing the *plaza*, a *mestizo* girl of great beauty—though it would not last many years—had cast an inviting look at him. He had looked back at her with an answering glint in his eyes which had made Francesca suspect that, with women, he might be as ruthless as most men.

'Shall I deal you in, Paco?' he asked.

She shook her head. 'I don't play. May I look at your books?'

'By all means, but I'm afraid I can't offer to lend you any. I'm leaving here some time tomorrow.'

Her father said, 'Paco tells me you've lost your crew. He's a boy who can make himself useful. Perhaps you might care to consider signing him on for a short spell. We've also been thinking of leaving, but most of the boats plying this river leave a good deal to be desired in the way of passenger accommodation. A space on the deck, among the livestock, is usually all they can offer.'

Caspar Barrington picked up his hand and considered the cards he had drawn for some moments before he replied, 'I'm sorry I can't oblige you. I never carry passengers and, as far as the lack of a crew is concerned, I can handle *Rain* single-handed in all but the worst weather conditions, and they don't arise on a river passage.'

'Oh, come now, old man—surely you won't refuse to help a compatriot out of a difficulty? We should be no trouble, I assure you.'

'You are troubling me now,' said his host. He reached out and took the *cheruto* which was smouldering between Andrew's fingers and, opening a fly-screen, tossed it out into the river. 'I'm a non-smoker,' he explained curtly.

'I'm sorry . . . why didn't you say so?' was Andrew's response, in a tone of grudging apology.

'Why didn't you ask before you lit it? It's the usual form among those who are *todo un señor*, as your son described you to me earlier.'

Caspar Barrington's sarcastic inflection was accompanied by a glance of undisguised contempt for the other man's kippered forefingers, his pomaded hair arranged to camouflage his baldness, the dandified silk bandanna flowing from his breast pocket, and his quivering hand reaching out to pick up his glass.

His scorn made Francesca flush scarlet, and she longed to spring up, and say, 'Father, I think we should leave now.'

But although, unlike him, she had no objection to travelling down-river with goats and chickens and probably lice as her companions, there was no guarantee that by the time the supply boat arrived they would still have the money for their fares.

Already her locket—her only memento of her mother—was in the hands of the hotel-keeper, and could be reclaimed only if they gave him most of the money Caspar Barrington had paid for the paintings.

Whatever it cost her in humiliation, either on her own or her father's account, she would willingly humble herself if it enabled her to recover the little gilt case, on a

necklet of shabby black ribbon, which contained a miniature, delicately painted on ivory, of her Italian grandmother as a young girl.

Either Andrew did not recognise it, or he chose to
ignore Caspar Barrington's sarcasm. 'You must forgive
me, my dear chap. Living among all this riff-raff'—with a
gesture in the direction of the quay—'one tends to fall
into their ways. It's partly a matter of protective colour,
you understand. It doesn't do to let them see one has
been accustomed to better things. Makes 'em suspicious
and hostile. As a painter I find them fascinating; as a
man, I don't trust them an inch. They would slit my
throat in a moment if they thought there would be any
profit in it.'

'But you don't consider it necessary to dress in the
manner of your son?'

Caspar Barrington's glance contrasted her patched and
darned cotton garments with Andrew's bespoke tussore
suit, years old but retaining the hallmarks of expensive
tailoring.

Francesca said quickly, 'I'm still growing, and I mess
up my clothes. My father is only wearing his best suit as a
gesture of courtesy to you, *señor*.'

'I see.' His gaze rested thoughtfully on a threadbare
place she had darned. 'You appear to enjoy the services
of a first-rate needlewoman. I'm not a bad mender
myself, as most sailors have to be, but I can't compete
with repairs of that order. It might have been done by
the tailor of Gloucester's helpful mice—but perhaps you
don't know that story?'

'I don't think so. Who is it by?'

'A woman called Beatrix Potter whose tales and drawings are familiar to most English children.'

'I'm only half English,' she answered, expecting to see
in his eyes the same flicker of scorn she had seen when he
looked at her father.

Naturally he would assume that the other half of her

breeding was South American Indian, and she had long been familiar with the disdain of the pure-bred for anyone of mixed stock; even though in her observation, the children of miscegenation were often more handsome and graceful, and always a more beautiful colour, than either white or black people.

Strangely he gave no sign of thinking the thoughts she ascribed to him, although the intent look he gave her made her bend her head over the book she had taken from the shelf built in behind the banquette.

Perhaps if he knew I was a girl, he would take us with him, she thought. But even as she considered the possibility of confiding in him, she remembered, with an inward shudder, the night she had overheard a conversation between an old French priest and her father.

She had been younger then and, in the eyes of all decent men, still a child, happy sewing dresses for a china doll called Jemima.

The priest had spent a long life in every part of South America from Colombia in the north-west to Argentina in the south. He had worked in the shanty-town slums outside the great cities like Rio de Janeiro, and survived more than one revolution. He had warned the Englishman that in many ways South America had as much claim to be called the Dark Continent as had Africa. He had spoken of vices long since eradicated in Europe, but still not unknown where they were; of young virgins and even little girls kidnapped and sold into horrible slavery.

She had not understood everything he said, but the seed of a deep-rooted terror had been implanted in her mind; a fear reinforced when, the next day, her father had taken away the doll, hacked off Francesca's thick, waist-length pigtail and told her that, from now on, she must pretend to be a boy.

Since then her mistrust of all men had increased, not only because, as time went on, the masquerade became more difficult, but also because of her father's diminishing power to protect her.

Until the arrival of Caspar Barrington, she had never felt anything but apprehension when any member of the male sex took more than the most cursory notice of her.

Her reaction to him was more complex, and she could not analyse her feelings. But although she saw things to like in him, her instinct for self-preservation told her that merely because he was an Englishman, and clean and educated, it did not mean he was trustworthy.

He could be one of the many criminals who sought refuge in South America. He could be a most evil man who, if he found out her secret, would not scruple to murder her father before raping her, and leaving her with a choice between drowning herself in the river or joining the wretched girls in the town's squalid *casa de putas*.

Her thoughts made her quake with horror, and ache with unbearable longing to be part of that world where girls grew up safe and sheltered, in comfortable homes with ordinary, respectable parents.

It was a world glimpsed from afar but never experienced. Even in their comparatively palmy days in Mexico and Central America, they had never stayed long in one place, nor had Andrew's relationships with women ever lasted more than six months.

Now, unaware that what many of her contemporaries craved was freedom, Francesca hungered for security.

The men played cards for an hour, and it was as well that no money was involved because, as usual, her father was out of luck.

Normally, like most heavy drinkers, he could imbibe for a long time before becoming visibly tipsy. Tonight, however, when Caspar went to the galley to make some more coffee, Andrew suddenly fell asleep. Try as she might, Francesca could not awaken him.

When Caspar came back, she said uncomfortably, 'My father's had a long day. He . . . he hasn't been very well lately, and he usually goes to bed early. I should like him

to see a doctor, but there isn't one here. Please . . . *please*,
Mr Barrington, couldn't you stretch a point and give us a
passage, just as far as the coast?'

'I'll take you to the coast, if you like. But not him,' was
Caspar's reply.

'W-what do you mean?' she stammered nervously.

He said, 'I feel sorry for you, Paco. Life's given you a
raw deal. I'm prepared to take you as far as the nearest
British Consul; but your father—no! I'm not going to
encumber myself with a drunkard.'

'But I couldn't leave him,' she protested.

'Why not? He's done nothing for you, apart from
giving you life, and any fool can do that. Stay with him
and you're sunk. Come with me and you can begin
living.'

She watched him pour out the coffee. 'You're a hard
man, *señor*. Very hard.'

'I'm a realist,' he said, with a shrug. ' "Man that is
born of a woman is of few days, and full of trouble." So
he should make the most of his "few days". Do you know
where that quotation comes from?'

She shook her head.

'It's from the Old Testament of the Bible, which con-
tains the most beautiful language in English literature.
It's part of your heritage . . . denied to you by your
father. Let him go his way. You go your way.'

'No, I couldn't leave him . . . I couldn't! He needs me.
How could I leave him?'

'That's a woman's attitude, *chico*. A woman needs to be
needed, but a man has his own way to make. You've
trailed round with him long enough. If you hang about
here much longer, it'll be too late to catch up the years
that you've lost . . . the years when you should have been
at school, exercising your brain and competing with other
young people.'

'But how could I live without Father? We have no
relations in England—no one who would take me in,

even if I had the money to get there.'

'The Consul would organise that. Once you were
there, the State would provide. It takes care of plenty of
people well able to stand on their own; there should be no
difficulty in obtaining help for someone in your shoes.'

'But I shouldn't fit in there, in England. I shouldn't
belong,' she said flatly.

'You don't belong here,' he returned. 'And however
lonely you might feel at first, you wouldn't be destitute—
which is what you're going to be here, when your father
has drunk himself into an early grave.'

'Oh, don't say that!' she exclaimed distressfully.

'Not saying it won't alter the facts. In this climate, too
much alcohol is lethal. Only fit men survive. I'd say your
father had about twelve months, at most. Then you'll
have to face life on your own, so why not now? It's even
possible that the shock of your leaving might make him
pull himself together—although I shouldn't bank on it,'
he added cynically, his lip curling as he looked at the
lolling, open-mouthed figure of the sleeping artist.

'You must be very cold-blooded to suggest that I
should leave him here to die on his own. Would you leave
. . . have left your own parents in similar circumstances?'

The planes of his face seemed to harden. His eyes
looked colder than ever. He said harshly, 'I would never
allow anyone, of any relationship, to become an encumbrance upon me. A man's first duty is to himself—to
live his own life to the full, not to martyr himself for
someone else, particularly someone unworthy of such a
sacrifice.'

His philosophy chilled her. She sensed that here was a
man as strong and self-disciplined as her father was weak,
and who felt not one ounce of compassion for people
more frail than himself.

'But surely if one is fond of someone——' she began.

He shrugged. 'That's something I know nothing of. But
to mislead yourself into thinking you feel an affection for

him'—with a nod at her father—'strikes me as as great a
folly as when a man and a woman who are sexually att-
racted elevate their desire into "love". If you don't wish
for any more coffee, I'll help you get him back to the
hotel.'

Andrew did rouse when Caspar shook him, but his
movements were those of someone heavily inebriated, and
Francesca could never have managed to get him to their
room on her own. She could only suppose he must have
been drinking again while she was out on her errands.

Having hauled him ashore and supported him across
the *plaza*, at the foot of the staircase in the hotel Caspar
pushed him up two or three steps and then let him slump
over his shoulder. Her father's unintelligible protests
made Francesca cringe with shame for him. When they
reached the first landing, she slipped past and hurried
ahead to unlock the door of their room.

After seeing the comfort and cleanliness on board the
sloop, she hated Caspar to see the dingy garret with its
two sagging beds and the cracked and discoloured wash-
basin which was their living-place.

'Which is his bed?' he asked her, when he arrived at
the threshold, his breathing not even quickened by the
exertion of carrying the other man up the three flights of
steep stairs.

'That one.'

As she watched him deposit her father on the creaking
springs, she murmured a chagrined, 'Thank you . . . I'm
sorry about this.'

'*You* have nothing for which to apologise. Do you wish
me to undress him?'

She shook her head, plumbing the depths of a humiliation worse than any she had known.

Moving back to the door, Caspar checked. 'Think it
over—my offer to take you down to the coast,' he advised her gravely.

She made one last desperate appeal, knowing before

she spoke that it was hopeless.

'There are several more pictures here. You can have them all, free, and welcome, if only you'll change your mind. Please, Señor Barrington ... please ... won't you have pity on us?'

'I have some for you—none for him,' he answered. 'If I had taken pity on every drop-out and misfit I've met in the past two years' sailing, *Rain* would have sunk under their weight. Goodnight.'

He went out and closed the door, and she heard him going down the stairs, his footsteps surprisingly light for so tall a man.

CHAPTER THREE

FOR Francesca it was a night of little sleep.

Although her reason acknowledged that everything Caspar had said to her was true, and she longed with all her heart to escape not only from this place, but also from the man who had killed every spark of affection in her; yet her conscience could not accept the idea of abandoning him.

At the same time her courage faltered at the thought of finding herself abandoned if Caspar was right in suggesting that her father's health could not hold out much longer against a continued excess of cheap liquor.

Thinking about Caspar, and his obdurate refusal to take Andrew Hartley as a passenger, she wondered what lay behind his strange remark that filial affection was an emotion unknown to him.

To the affection between men and women he was also a stranger, it seemed; and indeed Francesca herself had never encountered, in life, the love described in the books which, from time to time, came her way.

Sometimes, in a maudlin mood, her father would speak as if his love for her mother had been the transcendent experience of his life, and her death a blow from which he had never recovered. But somehow his daughter could not believe that being widowed was the real reason why he sought refuge in drink.

As for herself, she had always been too preoccupied with the necessities of life—food and shelter—to spare many thoughts for young men; and although once or twice she had seen a youth who had drawn her eyes with his physical beauty, her disguise as a boy meant that no heterosexual men gave her a second glance.

When the dark, stifling night at last gave place to the dawn, she slipped out of bed and through the much-mended folds of the dingy mosquito net. With a room to herself, she slept naked. Now, forced to share with her father, she wore a length of cheap cotton stitched into a tube, and folded and tied like a sarong.

Stitching the seam had given her the rare pleasure of using her needle on new material. When Caspar had noticed the fineness of the darning on her clothes, he had touched on her deepest frustration. From quite early in childhood she had felt a creative impulse to make things with her needle. The sight of bolts of bright fabrics on a market stall made her fingers itch to cut and sew.

But, apart from the fact that they could not afford to buy sewing materials, her masquerade precluded the activity. The prying woman who was supposed to clean the room, but who never seemed to make much improvement to it, would have been sure to discover any needlework, however carefully concealed. And what was the point of making things which could not be worn? So it was only in her mind that Francesca could fashion the delicate blouses and flounced skirts in which she would have liked to dress, given a free choice.

Before she stepped on to the balcony to breathe in the

early morning air—the only time of the day when a slight freshness could be felt in the otherwise soporific atmosphere—she put on her shirt and trousers.

The *plaza* and quay were deserted, for such a climate made for sloth, and none of the local inhabitants were early risers. They went to bed late and rose late, although in that first hour of daylight it would have been possible to accomplish tasks which took two or three hours later on.

One person, however, was active, and that was the skipper of *Rain*. He was swabbing the decks, wielding the mop as expertly as any housewife, and whistling while he did it.

Francesca watched him. Although she had made her decision, and knew it to be the right one for her—however foolish he might think it—she could not repress a long sigh of regret. It would have been wonderful to be leaving with him later that morning, saying farewell for ever to a place she had never liked, and which now seemed like a prison.

Before her father was awake, she took from his now crumpled coat the money Caspar had paid him. Some—enough for their fares on the supply steamer—she rolled up very small and secreted in a place where neither he nor the cleaning woman was likely to discover it. Later she went downstairs to recover her locket.

'Your father has sold many paintings to the other Englishman?' the proprietor enquired, when she paid him their arrears of rent.

'Only two—and for a poor price. But enough to pay for our room until the next steamer arrives.'

'That may not be for some time. Perhaps I had better retain this as a security,' he said, keeping hold of the locket which he had taken out of his safe. 'With a man of your father's habits it is better to be on the safe side.'

'We shall not leave here in your debt,' Francesca said stiffly. 'Please give me the locket.'

'My wife has a fancy for it. I will buy it from you.'

'I'm sorry, it isn't for sale.'

'We'll see about that when you settle your final account.'

He would have replaced it in the safe, but a voice from behind her said quietly, 'Give the boy his trinket.'

The hotel-keeper was a bully who enjoyed making life a misery for those who could not defend themselves. A shouter and blusterer himself, nevertheless he recognised the authority in that soft-voiced command, and became as abject as his victims. The locket was passed over the bar without further discussion.

'Coffee for two, if you please,' was Caspar's second instruction, as Francesca turned a grateful face to him.

'*Si, señor*. At once. Please to take a seat while I attend to it.'

'May I see?' Caspar asked, holding out his hand for the locket.

She put it into his palm. With his other hand he drew out a chair for her.

Having looked at the entwined initials on the front of the case, he opened it and studied the miniature.

'Who is this? Your mother?'

There was no point in pretending the painted face had no connection with her. Even without the aid of a magnifying glass to reveal the details invisible to the naked eye, the likeness was unmistakable.

'My grandmother.'

'Of what nationality? Spanish?'

'No, Italian.'

'You said you had no relations in England. What about on the other side of your family?'

'I don't know. My mother's family didn't approve of her marriage. She ran away, and they disowned her.'

'They might take a different view of a grandson in need of assistance.'

'They might—if they're still alive, and if I knew where to write to them.'

'Surely your father must know? They must be people of standing. Miniatures were always the prerogative of the well-to-do classes, and particularly since the introduction of photographs.'

'Father still feels very bitterly towards them, because they refused to accept him,' she explained.

'Nevertheless you should make him tell you where they lived, and may still live. Their surname will be on your parents' marriage certificate, if he has it among his papers. You have a passport, presumably? Or are you still included on his?'

'Yes, I'm on his passport.'

'Hm . . . a snag, but no doubt not insuperable. If you make a note of his passport number, I daresay it won't be too difficult to get you some temporary papers from the Consulate.'

'The problem doesn't arise. I'm not coming with you, Mr Barrington. Not without Father.'

His black brows contracted. 'You're being very foolish and obstinate.'

Francesca met his scowl without flinching. 'I could never be easy, not knowing what had become of him.'

'And you think, when it comes to the point, I shall change my mind and take you both. You're wrong. I shall not,' he said curtly. 'I have certain rules of life to which I make no exceptions. You have half an hour to change your mind.'

'My mind is already made up. Like you, I have my own code which I can't break—or not if I'm going to be able to live with myself.'

He rose, looking down at her from his great height with a glitter of impatience in his eyes. 'Very well, it's your choice. I only hope you won't regret it.' He tossed a note on the table to pay for the coffee, and held out his lean brown hand. 'Goodbye—and good luck.'

'*Buen viaje, señor*—and thank you again for entertaining us last night.'

They shook hands. Although her grip was a strong one compared with that of most girls, she felt her knuckle bones grind in the power of his fingers.

As she watched him crossing the *plaza* with the long, easy stride of a man in perfect condition, the proprietor reappeared with the coffee.

'*El inglés* has gone?'

'*Si*. My father will drink the other coffee.'

She took the cups from him and, with a heavy heart, turned away to mount the narrow staircase.

Five days after the white sloop had glided round the bend in the river, Francesca followed *Rain* downstream, but with no hope of catching her up, for her own craft was a dugout canoe she had bought from a *mestizo* youth who was more Indian than Spaniard.

Whether it was madness to set out in such a manner was something she would not discover until she reached the river's mouth, or failed to reach it. But after the bitter irony of her father's death by a stroke, only forty-eight hours after Caspar's departure, she was sufficiently desperate not to care very much what became of her.

Her first day on the river was uneventful but tiring. She was not accustomed to paddling, and it made her shoulders and back ache.

She spent the night moored to the end of an overhanging branch where she hoped to be safe from attack by any wild creatures. Even so, she was very much frightened, and slept in brief snatches disturbed by the strange night sounds of the river and the surrounding forest.

At sunrise, fortified by a cornmeal cake and cold coffee, she set off again, unrefreshed but glad to be on the move.

During the day she had the frightening experience of seeing an immense anaconda sliding into the river not far from where she was passing.

She knew that such snakes were not venomous, and

lived upon birds and animals. Nevertheless it was an alarming thing to see twenty-five or thirty feet of black and brown coils undulating into the water, and to recall hearing tell that such reptiles were capable of swallowing a goat whole, or even a cow.

She had hoped, by the second night, to have come to a riverside settlement. But the wide banks wound on and on with no sign of human habitation and, with darkness falling, she was forced again to tie up to a tree overhanging the water.

Once more, her sleep was disturbed by nightmares and alarming noises deep in the rain forest. It was when, wakened by a soft snarl from somewhere close by, she was lying awake, quaking with terror, that another sound broke the night's stillness—the mechanical purr of a motor.

For a long time she could not believe that the muffled throb was what it seemed: the noise of a boat under power. Was it coming up-river or down? She sat up, straining her ears.

A few minutes later she saw it, a smallish craft, moving upstream, midway between the two banks so that if she kept quiet it would pass her without the man at the helm noticing what might be a log in the shadows of the portside trees.

But she didn't keep quiet. Springing up, the canoe rocking wildly beneath her, she cupped her hands and yelled, 'Caspar! Ahoy, Caspar Barrington!'

Her desperate cries echoed strangely along the dark river. Then the glare of a searchlight swept over the current-swirled surface to fix on the dugout canoe and the small, frantic figure standing in it.

When Francesca woke from a deep sleep which she knew must have lasted for hours, she was lying in a comfortable bunk with a soft pillow under her head, and the bright gleam of water reflected on the deckhead above her.

For some time she lay without moving, searching her memory for a confused recollection of how she had come to be here, instead of in the cramped dugout.

Gradually her mind cleared, and she remembered untying the canoe and paddling towards the sloop. It had been an awkward manoeuvre, coming alongside and passing up the plastic-wrapped bundle which contained the rest of her father's paintings. Caspar had lifted her aboard as easily as if she were a child, and indeed she was several pounds lighter than when she had said goodbye, expecting never to see him again.

She remembered stumbling below, shivering with nervous reaction, and being given something to drink and a couple of tablets which she had swallowed without even asking what they were. Shortly afterwards, mental and physical exhaustion had swept over her like a great wave. Her last fuddled recollection was of toppling sideways on the banquette, and hearing his voice saying, 'That's right. You go to sleep, kid,' and then something else which had seemed to come from the far end of a long, long tunnel.

While she slept, he must have picked her up and carried her from the day-cabin to the cabin where she had awakened. Had he also removed her clothing? she wondered, with an agitated start.

But no, underneath the light covering which he had drawn over her she was still fully dressed. With a gasp of relief she relaxed, until the realisation of how filthy she was, how unfit to be lying on a clean sheet and spotless pillowcase, made her swing her bare feet to the deck.

It was now at least forty-eight hours, and possibly longer, since her last thorough wash. Although she had several times sluiced her face and hands with river water, the heat and the exertion of paddling had made her intolerably sticky, although she had not been conscious of it until now when, finding herself in cleaner and more civilised surroundings than she had known for many months, she felt as dirty and disgusting as a wharf rat.

But if she asked for a wash, Caspar would probably expect her to have it on deck in the sun, stripped, with a bucket, she realised worriedly.

From now on it was going to be extremely difficult, if not impossible, to conceal her sex from him. Men on their own, without the constraining presence of a woman among them, were much less selfconscious than her sex. She knew, from previous embarrassments, that they went about naked and performed various natural functions in front of each other with a free and easy casualness which women—except perhaps in the case of *putas* who had lost all normal feminine modesty—did not share.

If only she could be certain that, knowing her to be a girl, Caspar would treat her no differently, she would straight away admit her real sex. For surely if he were, in truth, *todo un señor*, to let him conduct himself as freely as he would with a teenage boy on board must be—when at last he found out—as embarrassing for him as for her?

Any nice man, she felt certain, would not enjoy the discovery that expressions and actions which were acceptable among his own sex had unwittingly been used and performed in front of a young girl.

But was Caspar Barrington a nice man? There was considerable evidence that he was not; notably his callous refusal to give her father a passage.

Suddenly, for the first time, it occurred to her to wonder why, last night, he had been travelling upstream. Could it be that he had changed his mind and been coming back for them? What other reason could he have had for retracing his passage?

But even if he had undergone a change of heart, and regretted leaving them behind, it still did not mean he was to be trusted to behave with unwavering chivalry if she revealed herself.

He was a man: a member of the strong, selfish, often brutal sex who for centuries had kept women in helpless subjection, and who, from what she had seen, still did.

Driven by the fierce and apparently uncontrollable appetite of his sex, he might not intend to harm her, but be unable to stop himself.

Not that, thin as she was and without the voluptuous curves which had made him leer at that other girl, she offered a man much temptation, Francesca thought wryly.

But at least she was a female, of his own race, and one he could take without any fear of the consequences; and that might be enough for him, particularly if he had been abstinent for a long time.

Her thoughts sent a shudder through her. She was safe from the perils of the river, but not yet totally safe. And was drowning, or being crushed to death by one of the great water snakes, any worse than the living death to which this man might commit her when he had done with her himself?

The door opened, and Caspar entered, making her blench. In the confined space of the cabin, he seemed even larger than before; a giant of a man from whom, instinctively, she recoiled.

'Ah, you're up. Good. Come and have lunch. After-wards you can have a shower, but I think food's your first need,' he said.

A savoury smell wafting from the galley made her rea-lise how famished she was, and his mention of a shower allayed, for the moment, her dread of confessing the truth to him. 'I—I must have slept round the clock,' she said, as he beckoned her past him.

'Yes, you might have done so in any case, but I gave you a couple of knock-out pills to make sure. You looked at the end of your tether.'

'Yes, I was pretty near it,' she agreed.

And closing her mind to everything but the thought of the first square meal she had eaten since her father's death, she obeyed his instruction to take her place at the table.

Hungry as she had been, Francesca was soon replete. Her stomach was not accustomed to large meals, nor had she a frame like Caspar's to fuel.

For her he had cooked an omelette filled with mushrooms; for himself a thick steak, also with mushrooms as well as fried eggs and potatoes.

They ate in silence. After his substantial main course, he had room for cheese and biscuits. But when he offered them to her she shook her head.

'Thank you, no. I couldn't manage another morsel.'

'Your appetite will improve in time. You could put on quite a few pounds and not be overweight.'

It was not until they were drinking coffee—Francesca's with milk, and Caspar's black, with brandy—that he leaned back against the banquette and said, with a measuring look, 'What possessed you to undertake such a foolhardy enterprise as following me in a dug-out?'

'I wasn't following you. I was trying to travel independently.'

'What! Down a hundred miles of river? You must be crazy! To refuse my offer to take you, and then to attempt it on your own . . . Did you leave without telling your father what you were planning, for God's sake? Or is he so lost to all sense—'

'He's lost to everything now. He's dead,' she said, in a flat voice. 'I thought his behaviour was strange the night we had supper with you. Usually he could hold his liquor much better than that. He must have been ill then, I suppose. He seemed all right the next day, but the day after that he collapsed. *Una apoplejía*, they called it.'

She wondered if, in spite of all his animadversions against her father, he would have the hypocrisy to condole with her. But Caspar's response was consistent with the lack of conventional sentiment that seemed to be characteristic of him. He said bluntly, 'A shock—but better for him and for you than a long illness miles from any proper medical facilities.' He did not dwell on the subject, but went on briskly, 'If you've finished your coffee, I'll show you how the shower works.'

She had intended to ask him what had changed his mind and made him return up the river. But while she was under the shower, revelling in the creamy lather from the cake of refined English soap which she found in the soap tray, she decided to say nothing.

Strange, cold-hearted man that he seemed, he might prefer not to admit to having broken one of his own "rules of life". She wondered what other rules he had made for himself.

It was years since she had felt as clean as she did when she emerged from the shower compartment, dried and dressed in a clean shirt and a pair of trousers of her father's which she had brought with her because they were in better condition than her own clothing.

The hotel-keeper's wife had professed to be shocked on seeing her in garments which had belonged to the dead man. But Francesca suspected that this was only because, although they were of no use to her paunchy husband, Señora Gomez had hoped to profit from Andrew's belongings, such as they were.

Perhaps a person more squeamish than she was would have shrunk from wearing them, Francesca acknowledged to herself. But life had never allowed her to develop delicate sensibilities, and Caspar was not the type to look askance when she appeared in her father's clothing. He had been a lightly built man, not much taller than his child, so his clothes were only slightly too large for her, and that, for as long as she could maintain her subterfuge, was all to the good.

In spite of her nervous misgivings, in the next few days nothing happened to expose her. She slept a great deal of the time, not only at night but for many hours during the day. She had never felt so tired before, and supposed it must be a reaction to the years of tension and uncertainty.

The day before they expected to reach the mouth of the river, and the city where Caspar would hand her over to the Consul, he surprised her by saying suddenly, 'I think you could do with a period of acclimatisation—psychological rather than physical—before you're transplanted to Europe. Would you like to stay aboard *Rain* as far as Antigua?'

She could scarcely believe that he meant it.

'Could I? Oh, yes, *please*!' she answered.

'But there'll have to be less of this snoozing once we're at sea,' he warned her, for she had not long wakened up from a long nap under the awning.

This, while they were moving under power rather than sailing, remained hoisted all the time, its shade a welcome relief from the burning tropical sun which made the wide river glitter with almost painful brilliance.

'Oh, no. I'll make myself useful. You won't regret it, sir. Thank you . . . thank you,' she said fervently.

'There's no need to call me sir, as long as you always do what I tell you, when I tell you.'

He went below, leaving her to hug herself with delight at this unforeseen reprieve from being left on her own among strangers.

It was a long time since Francesca had last seen the ocean, and for several hours after they had emerged from the delta the water slapping the sloop's hull was murky with detritus washed downstream by the great river. But it smelt like the sea, in spite of its cloudiness, and the fresh salt tang of the breeze soon washed away the last trace of the miasma of the mud-flats and the dank, heavy smell of the rain forest.

'Why is your boat called *Rain*?' she asked him, that first night at sea, when they were scudding north, and she was with him in the cockpit.

At first she thought he had not heard her, or had heard but chose to ignore the first personal question she had ventured to ask him.

But after a pause he answered, 'She was bought with a rain of diamonds.'

'A rain of diamonds?' Francesca had no idea what he meant by that reply.

'Have you ever heard of Queen Victoria?'

'Of course. She ruled England for sixty-four years, from 1837 to 1901, and she had six Prime Ministers— Melbourne, Peel, Palmerston, Disraeli, Gladstone and Salisbury.'

'Where did you learn all that?' Caspar asked, on an amused note.

'I'm not completely uneducated. We used to have a one-volume encyclopaedia. Having nothing much else to read, I read that, and certain facts stuck.'

'I see. Well, in the first twenty years of Victoria's reign, precious stones, particularly diamonds, were sometimes set in a waterfall, that's in straight bands of stones arranged side by side, and sometimes on separate stalks, in which case they were known as a "rain". When I was twenty-one, an old lady left me a rain of diamonds which had belonged to her great-grandmother. I sold it to pay for this boat, and named her after the jewel which had made her possible.'

'A rain of diamonds,' she murmured, half to herself. 'It must be a beautiful thing.'

'No more beautiful than moonlight on a calm sea, or the spray flying up from the bows. And diamonds are mined in conditions to which most of the people who wear them never give a thought,' he said harshly. 'It always amuses me to read of women refusing to wear certain furs, or to use certain cosmetics, because they cause suffering to animals. They don't stop wearing gold chains, although gold is mined by human beings in conditions I shouldn't care for.'

His tone made her wonder suddenly if, when he said "women", he thought of one particular woman.

The next day, late in the afternoon, they put in close to

the coast, to a bay where the water was clear, and the colour of an aquamarine Francesca had once seen in the crown of a Madonna in a cathedral.

Caspar would not let her swim because there were sharks in the area.

'But we can haul up buckets of water for a salt-water shower in the sun,' he said, when the sloop was at anchor.

The moment she had dreaded had come.

A boy, in her place, would have stripped off his clothes and enjoyed being douched with buckets of water. What was she to do now? she thought, frantically searching for some excuse. Caspar himself had been stripped to the waist all that day, and she had been expecting him to chide her for keeping her own top half covered. But he had said nothing until now.

She watched him unzip his shorts, revealing beneath them a pair of brief, bright green underpants, or perhaps they were up-to-date swimming trunks. Certainly they bore no resemblance to her father's loose-legged poplin undershorts. These were made of a fabric like towelling, but with the ability to stretch, for the briefs hugged Caspar's muscular buttocks as closely as a second skin, sitting low on his lean male hips and emphasising the litheness of his waist and the length and strength of his thighs.

He folded his shorts and turned. 'Get a move on, lad. What's the matter?'

'I . . . I . . .' Her throat was dry, her face scarlet.

Caspar's grey eyes narrowed, and he gave a short sardonic laugh.

'Do you really imagine I don't know your secret, *chiquilla*?' he asked mockingly, emphasising the feminine ending of the word which was almost the same when addressed to a male adolescent. 'I guessed it almost immediately. It was only because I knew the truth about you that I changed my mind and turned back up the river.'

'H-how did you know?' she stammered huskily.

'My dear girl, almost everything about you gives the game away. Not to these people, perhaps'—with a jerk of his head towards the land—'but certainly to any Englishman with reasonable powers of observation. What's your real name?'

'Francesca.'

'I wondered if it might be. A pretty name, that goes better with long hair and skirts than with that shaggy mop and those clothes. From now on you can be a girl again.' He put out his hand to take her firmly by the chin and tilt her flushed face up to his. 'Perhaps not a bad-looking one when you've learnt all the tricks of your real sex.'

He let her go, passed her and went below. A few moments later she heard him call, 'Come here, Francesca.'

With lagging steps she moved to obey his command, remembering the terms on which he had kept her aboard—'as long as you always do what I tell you, when I tell you.'

Caspar was not in the day-cabin.

'W-where are you?' she called out timidly.

'Here . . . in the spare cabin.'

She began to tremble. Hers was a twin-berth cabin, as was the one which he occupied. She had glimpsed it during the day when the cabin doors were hooked back for greater airiness between decks. But the spare cabin had a wide berth in which two people could sleep together, if not with quite as much room as in a double bed ashore, with much greater freedom of movement than were they to share an ordinary berth.

She approached the doorway, distraught with an uprush of terror. For years, ever since the priest had talked to her father, she had been haunted by the fear of being taken by force; of being changed from a girl to a woman not with love and gentleness, but by a cruel act of rape which would leave her defiled and abased.

'P-please ... I beg you ... don't hurt me,' she pleaded, standing by the coaming, her hot cheeks now pale with fright, her thin hands clasped tightly together.

'Hurt you?' Caspar said blankly.

He was sitting on the edge of the berth, in the act of pushing back a locker which rolled out from under the mattress.

Her panic was too all-consuming for her to be conscious of anything but the near-naked, brown-skinned body of the man in whose power she had placed herself.

As he rose, she shrank back with an incoherent cry for pity.

'What on earth's the matter with you, girl? Here you are ... I've found a bikini for you. It was left by one of the parties who chartered the boat some time back.'

As he held out the bright bits of cloth, there was a hiatus in which he was swifter to understand her than she to grasp her mistake.

'Mother of God! What kind of brute do you take me for? You're a child still ... a skinny kid!'

'Th-there are men who——' She started to weep.

Not for years had she shed one tear, and now they poured down her cheeks too fast to be wiped away by her unsteady fingers.

Breathing with long shuddering gasps, she was scarcely aware of being bundled back to the day-cabin and made to sit down on the banquette. A few seconds later he gave her a clean gingham napkin in which to bury her face while she strove to pull herself together.

'Listen to me,' he said quietly, when at length her sobs had subsided, although she kept her face hidden.

'There are men like those you're afraid of, but I'm not one of them. You're as safe with me as with your father—safer, since I can protect you better than he could.'

As she raised her wet face from the napkin, her thick lashes spiky with tears, Francesca saw a faint smile tilt his mouth.

'Now don't go getting hold of the wrong end of that stick, my child. I like women as much as any man— grown women with breasts and hips, not immature twigs such as you are at present, *chiquilla*. When you're, let's say, nineteen, and a nicely rounded size twelve, you may have something to worry about. But that's a few years off yet, and meanwhile you can regard yourself as my little sister.'

He paused before adding, 'In fact it might be a good thing, if we run across any other Europeans, to pass for brother and sister. Not because anyone raises an eyebrow at a grown-up girl crewing for a man nowadays, but you're not grown-up, and I shouldn't want anyone else to credit me with the unpleasant inclinations of which you suspected me just now.'

'I'm sorry,' Francesca said tremulously.

The kindness and understanding of his tone had been quite different from his previous manner. She would not have believed him capable of speaking in that gentle way. It was a revelation of a side of his nature she had thought did not exist.

'I'm going back on deck,' he said, more briskly. 'When you've collected yourself, go and try on that bikini. It should fit you fairly well. The woman it belonged to didn't have much flesh on her bones.'

Presently Francesca found that the bikini was not a bad fit. A tag stitched into one of the seams of the bottom half bore the number 8. Arranging the triangles of the top half over the slight curves of her bosom, she wondered how long it would be—if ever—before she achieved the size twelve which Caspar appeared to consider the proper shape for a woman.

He had spoken as if nineteen was an age she would not reach for a long time. Clearly he thought her very much younger than she was.

When she joined him on deck, some time later, and he saw the pallor of her body compared with his own, he said bluntly, 'You look like something that's been living under a stone, girl. You'll have to take care not to burn.'

Even her face and hands had never been really brown before, for the hinterland heat of South America turned people's skins yellow rather than brown. But within a few days of her starting to wear the bikini, the sea air had changed her jaundiced look to a warm honey-gold, and the parts of her which had been pallid were beginning to alter as well.

At the end of ten days at sea, her green eyes held a new sparkle, and she had begun to eat almost as heartily as Caspar, although, since her days were now full of vigorous activity, this did not make her any more rounded.

She worked hard at learning to be a good crew, below as well as on deck. At night, after supper, they both read. Caspar was reading a massive work in four volumes, *The Decline and Fall of the Roman Empire* by Edward Gibbon, which he told her was one of the world's great books. It looked heavy going to her, but she could become deeply absorbed in his yachtsman's manuals and cookery books.

Sometimes, with her comfortable bed, her three appetising meals a day, her frequent showers and shampoos, and her new-found sense of security, she could scarcely believe life could be so good and so happy.

It troubled her that the loss of her father meant so little to her. But when she confided this to Caspar, he said in his usual incisive, down-to-earth manner, 'I shouldn't allow it to bother you. Regretting the past is one of life's most futile exercises, and constantly looking to the future is very little better. The right way to live is to make the most of the present.'

It was a piece of advice which clearly he practised himself, and much of the time she succeeded in following his example and closing her mind to the problems she would have to face when this golden voyage came to an end.

How long it would take them to reach Antigua, she did not know and preferred not to ask. Caspar had shown her a map of the whole scattered chain of islands which were thought once to have formed an isthmus between Florida and Venezuela.

'About two and a half thousand miles by ocean,' he had said, in answer to her question about the overall distance between North and South America. 'From the United States mainland to Trinidad is eighteen hundred miles by air.'

The map showed only the larger islands, but he also had many charts and these detailed every small cay and even large rocks. If all were included, the number of islands forming a crescent at the eastern end of the Caribbean would amount to more than seven thousand.

As far as Francesca could judge, the distance from Trinidad, lying close to the coast of Venezuela, to Antigua, near the centre of the group of Leeward Islands, was at least as far as the distance from the mouth of the river to Trinidad. So when the mountains of Trinidad appeared on the horizon, she did not feel too much cast down.

In the bustling streets of Port-of-Spain, Caspar took her shopping for clothes. He bought her a pair of red sandals for going ashore, two pairs of very short shorts, a blue denim skirt and several bright cotton tops.

None of the clothes was quite what she would have selected had she not been concerned to choose as cheaply as possible, or if she had had the self-confidence to stand out against the advice of the helpful middle-aged assistant in the dress department.

But when the woman commended a sun-dress which Francesca thought hideous, she did resist, telling Caspar she would rather make one for herself.

'If you think you can,' he said doubtfully.

'I know I can,' she assured him.

'Does the young lady need underwear?' the assistant suggested, addressing herself to Caspar, as she had done from the outset.

Her manner made Francesca feel like a not very bright twelve-year-old, and catching glimpses of her reflection in the various mirrors about the department did nothing to boost her morale.

Her hair had grown longer since the day she had begun to live as a girl once more, but it wasn't much of an improvement, for it wouldn't stay back from her forehead but fell forward in a thick thatch and looked untidier than ever, besides being uncomfortably hot on the nape of her neck.

'Yes, she'll need some briefs,' agreed Caspar.

Whereupon the motherly assistant conducted them to another department and explained to a younger and much more glamorous colleague that Missy had lost all her clothes and needed completely re-equipping.

Perhaps they thought she had been shipwrecked, Francesca reflected, gazing with envy at the pretty Trinidadian behind the counter whose eyes were skilfully painted to enhance their limpid golden depths, and whose long nails matched her red lips.

'And perhaps some bras for the young lady?' she asked, when the briefs had been chosen.

Caspar glanced at Francesca's chest which, compared with the opulent curves of the girl on the other side of the counter, was still almost boyishly flat.

'Do you want a bra?' he enquired.

She shook her head, feeling oppressed by her continued angularity. Even her cheeks were still hollow, in spite of the large meals she ate. Projecting bones seemed to be part of her nature, like those of a cat, except that a cat's bones were hidden under its fur. Her thin wrists and shoulders were not. Would she ever be pretty and cuddlesome?

Presently Caspar left her in the department selling patterns while he went on some errands of his own. Having already been measured by the woman upstairs, Francesca knew the size she required, and spent a pleasurable ten

minutes leafing through a big book of styles until she
found one she liked.

He had left her some money to buy the material she
needed, and any necessary equipment which she did not
possess and was not to be found in *Rain's* supplies.

She was ready and waiting when he came back for her,
three metres of sea-green cotton in a parcel under her
arm. Later, studying the pattern, she found on the back
of the envelope a table of standard size measurements.
To achieve Caspar's ideal size twelve, she had to put on
three inches round her bust and hips, and even more
round her waist, which was narrow, even for her present
size.

They did not linger at Trinidad, but moved on north
to Tobago, a smaller and more scenic island, twenty miles
to the north-east. A hundred years earlier, when planters
had had to sell land for no more than ten shillings an
acre, it had been bought by former slaves whose descend-
ants still farmed the rich valleys.

It was here, moored in the most perfect bay which she
had ever imagined, that they shared their anchorage with
a yacht party which included a New York divorcee called
Beverley Vogt.

Beverley, and her friend and hostess Rosemary, were
unlike any women Francesca had encountered before.
She was fascinated by the lacquered perfection of their
long nails, the care with which they applied protective
creams to every inch of their bodies before and during
sunbathing, for which they removed the tops of their biki-
nis.

They urged her to do the same, but Francesca de-
murred. Even if her curves had matched theirs, she felt
she would not have wished to expose as much of herself as
they did. They did not take off their jewellery but wore
their gold chains and their rings even while swimming.
But their swimming was different from hers; they never
dived from the deck, or swam under the water. That

would have spoiled their hair and their make-up, which
was always immaculate.

Their looks, their clothes and their health were all they
ever seemed to discuss. Sometimes, after listening to their
conversation, Francesca would question Caspar about it.

'Do many women in England have their hair coloured,
and their faces lifted, as soon as they begin to have a few
grey hairs and lines?' she asked him.

'It's a long time since I left England. I believe the
majority of older women had their hair dyed when I was
last there. I wouldn't know about face-lifts. Not many, I
shouldn't have thought, because of the cost of it.'

'Beverley and Rosemary speak as if everyone has it
done in America. Not only women, men, too.'

'Crackpots!' was his pithy rejoinder. 'I can understand
a woman wanting to keep her looks as long as possible,
but any man who's as worried as that about his appearance ...' The sardonic curl of his lip expressed his
opinion. After a pause, he asked, 'Have those two women
had face-lifts?'

'No, but Rosemary is thinking about it.'

'They must find the sight of you a little painful,' was
his response, accompanied by a gleam of rather cruel
amusement.

'Painful?' she repeated, not understanding him.

He did not explain for a moment, and then he said,
'The sight of a bud with the dew on it can't be very
welcome to a full-blown rose and one beginning to wilt
slightly.'

It was only when the gleam softened, and he stroked
her cheek with one forefinger, that she fully understood
the analogy: that she was the bud with the dew on it.

But even as his touch sent a little thrill of pleasure
through her, he turned away and went on deck, leaving
her surprised and happy. She had thought he might be
succumbing to Beverley's blatant attempts to charm him.
Now it seemed he was not interested in her after all.

All the rest of the hot, golden day she treasured his touch and the hint of affection in his voice. She even allowed herself to dream—without recognising the significance of her thoughts—that he might be waiting for the bud to uncurl her petals.

But that night, at a barbecue party on the beach, that idea was shrivelled by the sight of Beverley looking invitingly up at him, and Caspar looking down at her with an expression which made Francesca avert her eyes, all her earlier happiness spoiled.

The looks which they had exchanged were signals she had seen before when her vagrant life with her father had taken her into disreputable bars where the only other girls present were *putas*.

Their seductive smiles were put on like the paint on their pale, jaded faces. But in Beverley's case the provocative look must be genuine; and Francesca had seen too many men with the hot light of lust in their eyes not to recognise Caspar's reaction, and to feel it like a blow to the heart.

Her one comfort, during the night when she lay awake thinking about them, was that, much as Beverley might want him to be her lover, it was a desire very unlikely to be satisfied. There was nowhere they could be alone together.

The next morning the two American women decided to go to the beauty parlour in the Mount Irvine Bay hotel, while Rosemary's husband and her brother tried out the nearby golf course.

'Why don't you come with us, Francesca?' Rosemary suggested. 'Even if you plan to grow your hair long, it should still be trimmed regularly. It's lovely thick, healthy hair, but if you don't mind my saying so, honey, it needs attention from a good stylist. We'd be happy to have you come with us, wouldn't we, Beverley?'

'Surely—and Rosemary's right. Your hair is in great condition, but it does need shaping a little bit.'

Francesca needed no telling that her hair could do with some treatment to make it fall on her shoulders in the graceful tresses she had seen on girls advertising shampoos and tints in their American magazines. She had tried to improve it herself by chopping bits off with her nail scissors, but had only succeeded in making it look more unkempt.

Her eagerness to accept their suggestion was tempered by concern that it might prove unduly costly. Assured by them that it wouldn't, she then went to speak to Caspar, wishing it wasn't necessary to put him to yet more expense, yet longing to look more presentable.

There hadn't been time, in Port of Spain, to try to sell some of her father's paintings. But sooner or later they were bound to put in somewhere where a shop sold pictures and bought them, and then she would be able to repay all she owed him.

'Yes, have your hair cut by all means,' said Caspar, when she consulted him. He gave her some dollars.

Not long before the shore party were due to set out in the chartered yacht's power-boat, Beverley suddenly gave a groan of dismay.

'I can see whirling spots,' she explained, when her friend asked her what was the matter. 'You know what that means! In an hour I'll be flat out with migraine. I'll have to stay home and lie down, Rosemary.'

'We could go tomorrow instead.'

'No, no—you go right ahead. There's nothing you can do for me. I'll just take some pills and go to bed. With luck, I'll be better this evening.'

The others made sympathetic noises, but did not insist they must stay.

'What is migraine?' Francesca asked Rosemary, as the boat trip began.

'It's a very severe form of headache, with great pain and sometimes nausea. Beverley's had them for years. They don't seem to have any pattern. She was perfectly all right at breakfast.'

'Oh, yes, I know what you mean now. In Spanish it's called *la jaqueca*. I've met people who have suffered from it.'

Her reference to the language which for years she had spoken as often as her mother tongue prompted Rosemary to question her about her upbringing, and some of the American's enquiries were difficult to answer unhesitatingly.

They came back from the trip about four.

'Oh, good! Beverley must be feeling better,' said her friend, at the sight of two heads in the water between their anchorage and the beach.

Her husband steered in their direction, expertly cutting the engine to allow the boat to glide close to the bathers.

'Yes, I'm fine again, thank you. It wasn't a migraine after all, just a headache which went off quite quickly when I'd taken my tablets,' was Beverley's answer to their enquiries. 'My, how much, *much* nicer your hair looks, Francesca. Don't you think so, Caspar?'

'Considerably neater,' he agreed.

No doubt his brief comment and somewhat cursory inspection was consistent with his rôle as her brother, but it diminished her pleasure in the results achieved by the salon's principal stylist, whose skilful cutting and blowdrying had transformed an unruly mop into a medium-length bob with shape and movement.

It was while he was asking the other men what they had thought of the golf course that Francesca intercepted an exchange of looks between the two women which made it abruptly clear to her that Beverley's indisposition had been nothing more than a pretence. Clearly Rosemary had been a party to the subterfuge. Even if she had failed to recognise the stratagem from the outset, Francesca was not so obtuse that she failed to decode the older woman's raised eyebrows as meaning 'How did it go?' and the younger's response as 'Perfectly!'

The certainty that, during her absence, Caspar and Beverley had become lovers—since she knew of no better word for people who made love without their hearts being engaged—was a painful disillusionment.

Until then she had not realised how close she had come to forgetting the hard streak in Caspar which had made him turn down her father's request for a passage.

Because he had changed his mind later, and ever since had been kind to her, she had, foolishly, let herself forget that at the outset of their acquaintance he had struck her as a tough, ruthless man, possibly a man who was not in South America by choice.

Now, having known him for some time, she had all but dismissed the possibility that he might be wanted by the police. But even if there was nothing criminal in his past, there must be something he preferred to forget. If not, why did he never, ever, refer to anything which had happened before her time with him?

That night she had not been asleep for long when something woke her. At certain stages of her life she had slept as lightly as a wild creature, alerted by the slightest disturbance. Lately she had begun to sleep more soundly. But tonight, perhaps because she had gone to bed in a disturbed frame of mind, she found herself suddenly wide awake in the manner of former days, holding her breath while she listened for a repetition of whatever had wakened her.

When after a minute or two she had heard nothing, but was still convinced that she had not woken for no reason, she slid from her bunk and went to peer out of the port.

At first there seemed nothing to be seen, but some instinct made her keep watch. Presently, into her range of vision came *Rain*'s inflatable dinghy, being propelled by Caspar so quietly that the strokes of the paddle were scarcely audible against the ever-present murmur of the ocean on the reef.

Francesca saw him glide alongside the other yacht and hold the dinghy steady while Beverley, who must have been waiting in the shadows, climbed down to join him.

Telling herself that it should be a matter of indifference to her, but knowing that it wasn't, she watched them move out of sight in the direction of the beach. She guessed it would be nearer to dawn than midnight before they returned.

The next morning there was nothing in Caspar's manner towards her to indicate that he and Beverley were on a more intimate footing. That it was a mistake for her to advertise the fact by means of endearments and caressing gestures was made plain when, at lunch on board the other vessel, he suddenly announced that he and Francesca would be leaving during the afternoon.

Francesca felt sorry for Beverley then. She looked shattered.

It was Rosemary who said, 'So soon? Do you have to? Why?'

'We have an appointment in Antigua,' was his cool reply.

Later, when they had waved goodbye to the others, Francesca asked him when they had to reach Antigua.

'When it suits us.'

'But you said——'

'A white lie, *chiquilla*. One can have enough of other people's company, however pleasant they are.'

She felt impelled to say, 'You must be getting pretty tired of my company by now.'

'You're different. You make yourself useful, and you don't chatter as much as those two women.'

It was some time before the episode ceased to trouble her. Eventually she decided that although some people might condemn his behaviour, it had been Beverley and not Caspar who had engineered their brief liaison. Had she behaved more discreetly, perhaps it would have lasted longer.

Clearly he disliked any hint of possessiveness from a woman. Beverley should not have run a scarlet fingertip up and down his muscular forearm, or called him by anything but his name. In doing so, she had ended the interlude as surely as she had begun it. Of that Francesca was convinced.

CHAPTER FOUR

LONG afterwards, looking back on those halcyon weeks cruising slowly north through the Windward Islands, Francesca was able to recognise the chance that caused them to berth alongside a yacht called *Kestrel* as a happening of far greater significance than it seemed at the time.

She could never make up her mind whether the future was shaped by accident or destiny; but, whichever it was, she knew that the forces that directed the course of a person's life were seldom immediately recognisable when they occurred.

When, half asleep in the midday heat far up-river, she had heard Caspar's voice commanding her to come to him, she had had no intuitive intimation that her future lay with him—at least for a while.

Nor, when they put in at Marigot Bay, on the western coast of St Lucia, and the dock master directed them to a berth next to *Kestrel*, did she have any premonition that their few days' friendship with the owners was to have a more lasting influence than most of the fleeting acquaintanceships which they made at each port of call on their slow passage north to Antigua.

Marigot Bay had been a major location for the Walt Disney film *Doctor Dolittle*, and the focal point of the anchorage was Dolittles, a bar and restaurant built in an idyllic setting by the water's edge at the foot of a steep wooden hillside.

There was also a boutique and grocery, as well as a marine workshop and yacht chandlery. These amenities, combined with the natural perfection of the sheltered bay, made Marigot an excellent anchorage, although it had the reputation, among some yachtsmen, of being a place where thieving from boats was particularly rife.

However, the inner part of the bay, concealed from the sea by a spit of land thick with palm trees, was where Admiral Lord Rodney had at one time hidden his fleet during his successful campaign to wrest the island from the French, after it had changed hands thirteen times.

For his victorious battle off the Saintes, he had been rewarded with his peerage and a pension of two thousand pounds a year—a fortune in the late eighteenth century—and Caspar's interest in naval history made him willing to risk the possibility of pilferage.

The owners were not aboard *Kestrel* when Caspar and Francesca made fast. But they came back a little while later, and introduced themselves as Bill and Emmy Tate. They were Canadians, not young, but still full of physical energy and with warm, outgoing personalities.

They had been afloat for two years, since Bill's early retirement, and, having sold their home in Canada, were looking for a house in the sun as insurance against the day when they could no longer live on *Kestrel*.

'Now I'll tell you a thing which I think will interest you, Caspar,' said Bill, after inviting the newcomers aboard his schooner for a drink.

'We've been looking into the possibility of a home here, and we've learned that most of this coastline from the sea to a certain distance inland is what's known as *cinquante pas de la reine*. In English, they call it the Queen's Chain, and if anyone wants to build on it, they have to fix up a lease from Her Majesty Queen Elizabeth the Second.'

This led him to an exposition of the pros and cons of the island as a place to settle, and, perhaps having heard it before and feeling that it might not interest Francesca, his wife turned to her and began a separate conversation.

She was a domesticated woman, who made her own bread, even at sea, by putting the dough in a plastic bag in the sun to make it rise quickly. Having talked about cooking for a time, she turned to her other great interest, the embroidery of Mexico and the Central American countries they had visited while working their way round the seaboard of the eastern Caribbean.

Later, back on board *Rain*, Francesca said, 'I like our neighbours, don't you? But it makes me feel very uncomfortable, this pretence of being your sister.'

'Try looking at it from their point of view,' was his response. 'They're of the generation who try but can't really approve of younger people living together unless they're married. If they knew you and I were unrelated, it would offend their moral code far more than a harmless deception goes against the grain with you.'

'Does no one get married now until they've tried various partners?' asked Francesca.

Contemporary standards of behaviour were still something of a mystery to her. She could not relate the concept of romantic love embodied in poems and the classics with the casual changing of partners revealed to her by the more up-to-date books and the newspapers she had read recently.

Where was the connection between Browning's *Escape me? Never—Beloved! While I am I, and you are you*, or the feeling expressed in Shakespeare's love sonnets, and the trivial couplings of people in the public eye who seemed now to set the tone for everyone. Or did they? Perhaps the impression was a false one.

'Probably some people still do.' Caspar's tone was noncommittal. 'But to marry too soon can be a ruinous mistake.'

'You haven't ever been married, have you?'

It was the first intimate question she had ever ventured to ask him, and she was half afraid he might snub her.

But he only said, with curious vehemence, 'No, I always knew better than to commit *that* folly.'

His reply relieved her of a small and quite irrational weight which had lain at the back of her mind. She had disliked the realisation that, briefly, he and Beverley Vogt had been lovers. But somehow she found it more acceptable than the idea that, at some time in his mysterious past, he had loved a woman with his mind as well as his body, even if it had not been a love which had lasted.

'If we told them the truth, the Tates, don't you think they'd believe us?' she asked.

'They might, and again they might not. I prefer not to chance it.'

'Do I still look so young?'

His glance travelled briefly over her face and her figure. 'Not as young as you did. Still too young to be involved with someone of my age.'

'How old are you, Caspar?' she asked.

'Too old for you in the eyes of the Tates,' he said dryly. 'So however much it conflicts with your preference for truth, we'll keep up the pretence for the time being.'

That night they ate at Dolittles, going there in *Rain*'s dinghy which they moored at the restaurant's dock, and dining at one of the candlelit tables, outside by the moonlit water.

While Francesca was trying a coconut daiquiri—Caspar preferred his rum neat—and they were considering the menu, a party of tourists arrived in the ferry boat *Marigot Rose* which plied between that side of the bay and the jetty on the south shore where there was a road leading to Castries, the island's capital.

The tourists were English, a group of young men and

women who perhaps had come from a resort mentioned by the Tates with the lovely name of Anse Chastanet. The Canadians had said that Dolittles, unlike some Caribbean restaurants, did not require men to wear coats and ties after dark. It was a sailing people's place, and therefore informal.

However, the new arrivals were all dressed to the nines, with the girls in the latest fashions. Francesca gazed at them, fascinated by their clothes, hair and make-up, although she did not think much of the young men's manners.

They left the girls to seat themselves, not drawing out their chairs for them as Caspar always did for her, and ordering drinks for themselves before asking the girls what they would like.

Her critical thoughts must have been reflected in her expression.

'Are you wishing you were got up like that?' asked Caspar, for once misreading her mind.

'Oh, no! That's not what I was thinking—although I do like their clothes, especially the red dress,' she conceded.

'Then why the frown?' he enquired, with amused interest.

'Because their young men seem so churlish. You treat even your sister better than that,' she explained, with a sparkle of amusement.

He cast a thoughtful glance at the group at the nearby table. 'Perhaps they would be more gallant if their girlfriends were more feminine,' he said dryly.

'But surely they couldn't be more so?' she responded, puzzled.

'Femininity is more than a matter of low-cut dresses, high heels, long nails and heavy make-up, *chica*.' He still sometimes used this form of address to her. 'Girls who exhale like young dragons, and make noises like that little blonde'—this after one of the girls gave vent to a high

screech of laughter—'don't encourage solicitous treatment.' He turned his cool gaze on Francesca. 'Your
laugh I like, and so will a lot of other men.'

She could not help flushing with pleasure at the unexpected compliment.

To her even greater astonishment, he went on, 'It takes
more than feathers to make fine birds, of either kind. A
clear skin, and shining eyes, and a pretty mouth not thick
with goo, are more attractive to my sex than any amount
of fashionable packaging. You have all those assets—and
more.'

'H-have I?' she stammered, wide-eyed.

The candlelight gave his dark face a sheen like bronze
where the strong bones tightened the skin at cheekbone
and jaw, and over the proudly bridged nose. As his manners were different from those of the men with the girls, so
were his looks and his posture. Nowhere was there slack
flesh on Caspar, nor did he sit slumped in his chair.

'Have you decided what to have?' he asked, as a waiter
approached.

Confused by his praise, Francesca said vaguely, 'Oh
. . . you choose for both of us, will you?'

He ordered the pumpkin soup which was served with
home-baked banana bread, to be followed by Chicken
Marigot, a house speciality, with aubergine.

For dessert she had an ice flavoured with soursop.
Presently she wished she had had black coffee like
Caspar. When she looked up, in the middle of enjoying
the ice, she found him watching her with a look which
made her feel very young again.

Earlier, he had made her feel closer to womanhood
than childhood. Now—and by her own fault for choosing
an ice instead of coffee—she had put herself back in the
junior league, she realised vexedly.

'Good?' he asked.

'Delicious, thank you. I'm still trying to put on weight,'
she added explanatorily.

'You're nothing like as thin as you were.'

Both the words and his tone could not have been more impersonal had he been a doctor speaking to an underweight patient. It was almost impossible to believe that, before the meal began, he had praised her skin and eyes, and implied that her mouth was pretty.

That night, before going to bed, she spent a long time examining her reflection in the mirror screwed to the bulkhead. In spite of Caspar's derogatory comment on lipstick, she could not help feeling that the face she saw in the glass would be greatly improved by light make-up. But she had no money to buy any, and she could not ask Caspar for money when already he had done so much for her.

If only there was some way she could earn herself a little pin money!

The next night they dined with the Tates on *Kestrel*.

After an excellent meal, the two men volunteered to wash the dishes, and Emmy Tate fetched a box containing examples of the embroideries she had spoken about the day before.

The one which Francesca found the most interesting was a *mola* which Mrs Tate said was the work of the Cuna Indians of the San Blas islands off Panama. It was an oblong panel, intended to be sewn to the front of a blouse with another at the back, and the Canadian had been told that the work was thought to derive from body paintings of earlier centuries.

'I expect, as usual, it was the missionaries who insisted that the Indians wear clothes,' she remarked.

Francesca studied the way the embroidery was done. Boutique clothes had made her familiar with decorative shapes cut out and machine-stitched to skirts and beach bags. This was the process in reverse; several layers of bright cotton stitched together with the design cut away through successive layers, each one folded down and sewn under to show the colour beneath it.

On their third day at Marigot, after shopping for a take-away moussaka, recommended by the Tates, at the grocery store, she had a look round the boutique at the holiday clothes and souvenirs.

Afterwards, rowing back to the sloop, it struck her that with some left-over pieces of fabric given to her by Emmy, she might use the technique of the *mola* to make things that boutiques would buy.

The idea excited her so much that she spent half the night with the light on, snipping and stitching in a fever of creative activity. It was more absorbing and satisfying than anything she had felt since the dimly-remembered pleasure of dressing her dolls.

When she woke up the following morning she was almost instantly conscious of an unfinished project demanding her attention. Last night's work lay spread on the locker, not as good as she hoped to achieve, but not bad for a first attempt.

Later she showed it to Emmy, who was full of praise and encouragement. But Francesca said nothing to Caspar. She wanted to prove her wares saleable before confiding in him.

From Marigot they moved on to Castries where they stayed for some days, and where she had the frustrating experience of being told that her handiwork was good, but unacceptable in the small-quantity she had produced so far.

'Bring me a dozen of these beach bags in different designs and colourways, and we can do business,' said the owner of the first gift shop she tried.

Encouraged, Francesca next tried to sell some of her father's paintings and was shocked and, at first, disbelieving when the dealer she approached shook his head over them.

At first he was tactful in his refusal. Then, learning

they were not her work, he said bluntly that they were daubs.

He was not alone in his opinion. At each of the several places she tried, she was told the same thing. Her father's work was no better than that of a thousand competent amateurs, and the world was full of Sunday painters.

This was a much worse blow than if she had been told that her own work was no good. She had counted on selling the paintings to repay some of her debt to Caspar; a debt now increased by the sum he had paid for pictures he had not really wanted but had bought as an act of charity.

When she taxed him with it, he admitted he had not been impressed by her father's talent.

'But how am I ever going to repay you?' she muttered dejectedly.

'By working for me without wages when I start to charter again.'

'When will that be?'

'When I get back to Antigua.'

Francesca's face lit up. 'You mean I can stay with you? You aren't going to send me to England?'

'Not as long as you make yourself useful, and don't expect me to pay you.'

'Oh, no! I'll be *glad* to work for you. It will be a pleasure,' she said joyfully.

'Not always, my girl,' he said dampingly. 'There are many worse ways of earning a living, but it's not one long picnic. You'll see.'

But nothing he could tell her about the drawbacks of the charter game could reduce her relief and delight that Antigua was not, after all, going to be their last landfall together.

From St Lucia they cruised to Martinique, where she discovered that Caspar spoke very good French, and where they lingered for several weeks so that she was able to continue her needlework and sell some of it.

But when she tried to make Caspar accept the money she had earned, he refused to take it, telling her to keep it for pocket money. Eventually, realising that he was adamant, she spent it on buying more fabrics and trimmings.

It was in Dominica, the last of the Windwards, that Francesca met Harriet Scott-Leigh. They were introduced to each other by Harriet's daughter who, from a papoose-style sling on her mother's back, reached out a brown, dimpled hand to clutch at one of the beads which, knotted on a bright ribbon, were a trimming Francesca had copied from a sun-dress seen in a boutique for wealthy tourists.

Feeling the tug on her dress, she turned and smiled at the infant whose mother was standing close by her in the crowd round a market fruit stall.

'Hello, baby,' Francesca said softly. 'Do you like my beads? Are they pretty?'

The girl who was carrying the child glanced over her shoulder, exclaiming, 'No, no, Lucinda—let go! Oh, dear, I'm so sorry. Can you manage to prise her hand off it?'

Not without difficulty, for the bead hung behind her shoulderblade, Francesca managed to free it from the child's fist.

'What a darling! How old is she?' she asked, laughing off the mother's apologies.

There followed a conversation in which it emerged that the infant was one of three children, the other two being at home with their father—home, for the moment, being a ketch in the harbour.

'Only a holiday home, thank goodness, because much as I love it out here, I don't think I could cope permanently—not while the children are little. It's my husband's dream to live on the boat all year round, but we can't because of his job. So we have a month every winter. Are you here on holiday, too?'

'No, I live on a boat with . . . my brother. We're staying here for a while on our way north to English Harbour.'

'English Harbour, Antigua? That's where we've come from. It's *Sea Spray*'s berth when we're not using her. We have an agent there who arranges for her to be chartered as a bareboat when we're not aboard her, and the profits from that pay for our holidays. Do you and your brother charter?'

'Sometimes. Not at the moment.'

Presently, Francesca found herself helping Harriet to carry her more heavily laden baskets back to the ketch, and being invited on board to meet big, burly Sam Scott-Leigh, and the five-year-old twins, William and Alice.

She found them a charming family, and when Harriet said, 'Why don't you and your brother come and have supper with us tonight?' she would have been happy to accept.

'I'd like to, but I'm not sure if Caspar may have made other arrangements.' What she meant was that she was not sure if he would wish to spend an evening in such a strongly domestic atmosphere with small children underfoot. 'May I ask him, and let you know?'

'Of course. And you'd better warn him that it won't be a "gourmet dinner" as the Americans say. Just pot-luck and a bottle of plonk,' answered Harriet.

'Caspar—that's an unusual name. I used to be at school with a chap called Caspar, but he didn't have a sister,' said Sam. 'Incidentally, Harriet didn't introduce you properly. I don't know your surname.'

'Sorry . . . Hartley,' answered his wife, to whom Francesca had inadvertently given her real surname.

Suddenly she had a powerful premonition that the man she had referred to as her brother might be this man's sisterless school friend. He looked close to Caspar's age, and he had the same sort of voice, and something of the same presence as *Rain*'s tall, dark, commanding skipper.

'What was your friend's name?' she asked, steeling her-self not to show any sign of perturbation if his answer was what she expected.

'Barrington . . . Caspar Barrington, although he was always called Cub from the initials on his trunk.'

'I can't think of any boys' names beginning with U except Uriah and Ulric. Surely it wasn't either of those?' said Harriet.

'I think it was Upton,' said Sam. 'It's a long time ago. I've forgotten. But he was a nice chap . . . a good friend. I often wonder what happened to him.'

'You'll find out one of these days, when the dotty old grandfather dies and the solicitors start advertising.'

'I should think Cub has probably predeceased him. He was always risking his neck in some mad escapade. The chance of his making old bones is one in a million,' said her husband.

This exchange was baffling to Francesca, and she longed to discover the reason why Harriet had described Caspar's grandfather as "dotty", and why, and for what, when he died, the solicitors would advertise.

Instead she lifted Lucinda, whom she had been cud-dling, from her lap, and said, 'I must go. Thank you for the coffee, and I'll let you know about supper as soon as I can.'

Walking back to *Rain*'s berth with her basket, she won-dered if Caspar would want to meet the friend of his schooldays, or if he preferred to avoid all contacts from his past life, in the same way he avoided referring to it.

CHAPTER FIVE

CASPAR was not on board when she returned, and she busied herself with preparing their lunch. But while this occupied her fingers, it did not prevent her worrying in case Caspar should be angry with her for making the acquaintance of people whom he would prefer not to meet.

When she heard his light footsteps on deck, she braced herself to face his annoyance. And since to delay her announcement could only increase her nervousness, as soon as he came below she lost no time in saying quietly, 'Caspar, I'm very sorry, but something has happened which you may not like.'

'Oh? What have you done? Blown the housekeeping on some irresistible dress?' was his teasing response.

'No, of course not! Would I do that?' She was shocked that he should suggest it, even in fun. Her financial dependence remained a weight on her mind.

'Out with it, then. What infamy have you committed?' asked Caspar, opening a beer can.

'I haven't done anything really . . . except to fall into conversation with a girl whose husband used to know you.'

With the can tilted over a glass, he checked, his eyes suddenly wary.

'Used to know me? Where?' he asked crisply.

'At school—or that's what he says. Except that he doesn't yet know that my "brother" Caspar is the same as his friend Cub Barrington. You see, by a slip of the tongue, I told them my surname was Hartley. So he thinks you're Caspar Hartley, and his wife has asked us to supper. I—I said I would have to find out. So I can easily make some excuse, and we can leave here before they see you. I didn't mention our boat's name.'

He eyed her thoughtfully for a moment before he said, 'Why should I want to do that, Francesca?—To leave in a hurry without being seen by these people?'

'I don't know. I thought you might. You ... you sometimes give the impression of not wanting people to find out too much about you ... of being ... well, rather a mystery.'

'Say, rather, a self-contained man in a world where too many people are tiresomely eager to bore the most casual acquaintance with every detail of their physical ailments and mental hang-ups.'

Her green eyes were shadowed with anxiety as they studied his lean, tanned face. 'Is it only that?' she asked doubtfully.

'What else? Have you been worrying in case you'd thrown in your lot with a man on the run?'

'There must be cases of people who've done something they regret, which has made them outcasts—like the remittance men in the colonies in the old days,' she said, her lashes downcast.

'Not many cases, I imagine—and certainly not my own case. I'm neither a villain, nor a suitable subject for hero-worship,' Caspar said dryly. 'Was this man you met Sam Scott-Leigh?'

'Yes, it was. How did you guess? He can't have been your only school friend, although perhaps he was the closest?'

'Sam's father taught me to sail when I stayed with them once. The whole family was mad about sailing. It doesn't surprise me to find him somewhere like this. What's his wife like? You took to her, I gather?'

'Harriet? Yes—oh, yes, very much; and they have three adorable children.'

'Good God! Sam's a patriarch now. How unlikely,' Caspar said dryly.

'So we can accept their invitation?'

'By all means. I'd like nothing better. Where are they berthed? I'll go and say hello now.'

Francesca told him, and added, 'How will you explain who I am?'

'Very simply—by telling the truth. Don't wait lunch for me, *chica*. He and I may slope off to a bar if their boat is knee-deep in kids,' he said, disappearing on deck.

This was a turn of events which should have relieved and pleased her. Yet, eating a solitary lunch, she felt forlorn and deserted.

Presently she heard her name called, and put her head up through the hatch to find Harriet on the quay.

'Can I come and chat?' she asked, smiling.

'Please do. Where are the children?'

'They're staying with the men.'

'Caspar said they might go off somewhere.'

'No, they're baby-sitting, and swapping memories of their youth like a couple of octogenarians,' said Harriet, stepping aboard. 'Lucinda is having her nap, and the twins are being quiet with their colouring books—although that won't last long, I expect. But Sam will keep them in order. With me, they get out of hand sometimes, but they're always biddable with Pa.' She settled herself on a cushioned locker in the cockpit. 'Will it horrify you if I knit?'

'Why should it horrify me?' queried Francesca.

'In my shortlived spell as a career girl, I used to think knitting was the final surrender to middle-aged dullness. Now I find it curiously satisfying, although it's impossible to concentrate on a complicated pattern except when the children are in bed.'

Harriet produced from a plastic bag something being made with red mohair.

'If you're going to knit, I'll sew. I'll just go and fetch my work-bag,' said Francesca.

For a while, after her return, the two girls talked about clothes. Then, after a pause while she counted stitches,

Harriet said, 'Sam has often talked about Cub—Caspar,
I should say—and so has Sam's mother. She had a very
soft spot for him. I must write and tell her how nice he
is—not a bit dour and monosyllabic now he's grown up.
A considerable charmer, in fact, judging by first impres-
sions. I think she was always afraid he would go to the
devil, as her generation would put it. So she'll be very
pleased and relieved to hear that he hasn't.'

'Why should she have thought he might?' asked Francesca.

'It sounds to have been about as miserable a start in
life as any boy could possibly have—a father who drank,
and had been disowned by *his* father for making a bad
mésalliance,' was Harriet's reply. 'My mother-in-law
called on them once—Caspar's parents, I mean. It wasn't
curiosity on her part. She knew nothing about his strange
background. She went to return a sweater which he had
forgotten to pack after spending a holiday with her. She
knew his home was in Fulham, and she got the address
from the bursar's department. When she called, his father
was sozzled, and his mother—perhaps one can't blame
her—had become a downtrodden slattern. If it hadn't
been for Caspar's grandmother, who had some money of
her own to pay for his education, he would have grown
up with no respite from his parents' rows and his father's
incessant drinking.'

'I see. I didn't know that,' Francesca murmured.

So that was the reason for Caspar's adamant refusal to
become involved with her father: his own growing up had
been blighted by a man with a similar weakness.

'I wonder if he's still alive?' she said, speaking half to
herself.

'Caspar's father? No—no, he isn't,' Harriet told her.
'His death was reported in the papers about a year after
we married. We happened to be staying with Sam's
people at the time, and I remember my father-in-law
reading it out at the breakfast table. If Caspar's father

had died from natural causes, it would have passed without notice. But he was knocked down by a car, and there was an inquest at which it emerged that, although he was known as "Mr" Barrington, he was really Lord Newark, the heir to Lanyon—as Caspar has been since his death, of course.'

Francesca blinked at her. 'Lord Newark? Lanyon?' she said blankly.

'Didn't you know? Oh, why should you indeed? I don't suppose he ever thinks of it. Having been shunned by his grandfather, through no fault of his own, it's now his turn to shun the old man. Perhaps, having been out of England all these years, he doesn't even know that his father is dead now.'

It took time for Francesca to accept the idea of Caspar being the son of an English aristocrat—even one who had drunk and married badly.

'But how could his father be Lord Newark if *his* father is still alive?' she asked, her delicate brows drawn together in mystification.

'Because the old boy is a marquis—he's Lord Lanyon—and Lord Newark is the title of the heir. He's very old now, nearly ninety, and originally he had three sons. But the older two were both killed in the Second World War. Lord Lanyon had always been eccentric, but the grief of losing two sons sent him right round the bend. I believe that in *his* father's day—way back in the Edwardian period—Lanyon was immensely luxurious; the King and his set used to stay there. But now it's a ruin, so one hears. He lives there all by himself, with one decrepit old servant, and there've been no repairs since his wife's death, which must be ten years ago. If he lasts out much longer, it will only be fit for demolition. Probably it's that already. Great mansions fall into decay even faster than ordinary houses.'

'When his grandfather dies, will Caspar have to go back?' Francesca asked, with a troubled expression.

'He won't have to—no. Who could make him? I imagine it depends on what money there is, and whether it's entailed.'

'What does that mean?'

'The fortunes of some old families can only be left to the heirs,' the other girl explained. 'It's a way of protecting the succession. But when money isn't entailed, it can be left to a cats' home, or perhaps to some distant cousin. And that's the sort of thing the old man would probably do, just to be spiteful. But even if he doesn't, the State will demand a colossal amount in death duties, so Caspar can't win either way.'

She saw the worry in Francesca's eyes, and said, with a reassuring smile, 'He explained how you came to be under his wing. I'm sure you've no need to fret that he'll suddenly whisk off to England, leaving you in the lurch again. I've been chattering nineteen to the dozen. Now tell me something about yourself.'

So Francesca talked for a short time about her own history and, when she stopped, Harriet said, 'You and Caspar have a lot in common. You must understand each other far better than anyone could who had always been happy as a child.'

'Perhaps—but the difference between us is that he's been properly educated, and I haven't. Where were he and your husband at school together?'

In the light of what she had already learned, it no longer came as a surprise to hear that the two men had been friends first at a preparatory school, and then for five years at one of England's most famous public schools.

'I imagine it must have been Lady Lanyon who left him the rain of diamonds which later he sold to buy *Rain*,' she said. 'He spoke of her as "an old lady", but I think it can only have been his grandmother.'

Not long after this he came back, and Harriet returned to her own boat with a cheery, 'See you both later.'

Caspar's reunion with his friend had left him in an abstracted mood. Francesca did not intrude on his thoughts, having much to occupy her own mind.

At supper that night, on board *Sea Spray*, in spite of the other three's efforts to involve her in the conversation, she could not but be conscious that they had many things in common of which she knew nothing. The years of Caspar's voluntary exile from his homeland had not broken the bond which existed between him and Sam. They were almost like brothers, long separated but still linked by the strong ties forged in their formative years.

But for her presence, she felt, they would have talked more of those days. Harriet, too, was a part of that world, her elder brother being another of Sam's schoolfellows.

Perhaps Caspar sensed how she felt. Strolling back to their own berth, he walked with his hand on her shoulder. She knew it was nothing more than a gesture of camaraderie. Nevertheless it comforted her.

The Scott-Leighs had only recently begun their holiday and, in the days which followed, the four of them spent much time together.

One morning, within a week of the men's reunion, Francesca woke up to find a large carton on top of her locker which had not been there the night before. She had turned in earlier than Caspar, and he must have come into her cabin after she had fallen asleep.

Taped to the side of the carton was an envelope with her name on it. Inside this she found a birthday card. Caspar, having glanced through her documents before hiding them safely away with his own important papers, had remembered a date invariably forgotten by her father. Not for years had she had a birthday any different from all the other days of the year.

Her fingers trembling with excitement, she undid the carton and gave a gasp of delight when she realised what

it contained—a compactly-cased portable sewing machine.

'Caspar! Caspar!'

Rushing out of her cabin and seeing that the main
hatch was closed, which meant he must be between
decks, she dashed to the galley and then to the door of his
cabin. As she lifted her hand to rap on it, he put his head
out of the washroom, half his strong jaw bearded with
lather, the other side newly shaven.

'Oh, there you are. Thank you . . . *thank you*!'

She darted towards him, then checked as he pulled out
of sight, saying, 'Hold it a second. I've got nothing on.'

She waited in the gangway until he stepped into full
view with a towel wrapped around his lean hips.

'Many happy returns of the day,' he said, smiling at
her.

A few moments before her delight had been so intense
that she would have rushed at him and hugged him, but
the brief pause had curbed that impulse. She stayed
where she was, unable to express her overjoyed gratitude
because suddenly there was a lump in her throat and
tears in her eyes.

'My dear girl, what's wrong?' he exclaimed, when the
tears overflowed and her only sound was a sob.

She shook her head, unable to explain that nothing was
wrong. It was happiness which had overset her normal
controls. Unused to showing her feelings, and afraid he
might be embarrassed, she bolted back to her cabin.

She had snatched a tissue to mop the irrational tears
when, to her surprise and confusion, Caspar followed her
into the cabin.

'I'm sorry, you m-must think I'm mad. Crying because
you've given me the most m-marvellous present I've ever
had in my whole life,' she blurted, on an uneven breath.

Caspar turned her to face him, his hands warm and
firm on her shoulders which were bare above the top of
the sarong in which she still slept.

'It does seem a curious reaction.' His tone was amused, but his eyes were kind as well as quizzical. There was no masculine unease in the presence of feminine emotionalism in the way he folded her against him and smoothed the thick silky tangle of her uncombed hair.

After ceasing to masquerade as a boy, she had no longer sought to avoid all physical contact and, living together in the confined spaces of a boat, they had often brushed against each other. But the brief, casual touch of elbow against forearm, or knee against knee under the table, was not like finding her cheek pressed against the faintly soap-scented brown skin of his bare chest, with the whole of her body close to his.

They did not last long, those unexpected moments in his arms, but they made her realise how wonderful it must be for Harriet always to be able to take refuge in Sam's arms whenever she was upset or downcast.

And being held close by a strong man wasn't only an even more pleasant sensation than stretching tired limbs between clean sheets on an innerspring mattress, she discovered. It was relaxing at first, but after a moment it set up a different reaction.

There wasn't time to analyse those second-stage feelings before Caspar put her away from him.

'No chores for you today, shipmate. As soon as I've finished shaving I'll organise breakfast. What do you fancy? Bacon and egg?'

He was already out of sight and on his way back to the washroom as he called out this suggestion.

'Yes, please,' Francesca called back.

Then she turned to examine his present more closely, and to read the instruction book. As she did so, she knew something had changed. The world today was a different place from the world yesterday, and it couldn't be merely because she had gone to sleep seventeen and woken up eighteen.

The day before the Scott-Leighs had to return to Anti-

gua, they all went for a picnic on *Sea Spray* to a cove
which they had to themselves.

It was the happiest of days, and it ended with the four
adults going to dinner at a hotel, leaving the children in
the reliable care of a widow who lived on the island, to
whom Harriet had been given a letter of introduction by
a friend of her mother's in London.

To make the occasion—arranged a week in advance—
doubly exciting for Francesca, she had a new dress to
wear. The material had been a present to her from
Harriet who, when the younger girl had protested at the
extravagance of her generosity, had said, 'I've been
thoroughly spoiled all my life; first by my parents, and
now by Sam. Let me share a little of my good luck with
you. The moment I saw it, I knew it was perfect for
you—green and gold, like your eyes.'

The material was Indian, intended for wear as a sari.
One edge of the gauzy green silk had a wide border,
woven of gold threads.

Before Caspar's present of the sewing machine, it
would have taken a long time to make up the dress and
its lining, also provided by Harriet. With the machine,
and Harriet's helping with the fitting, it took only two
days.

Late in the afternoon, when the picnic was over and
they returned to their own boat, Francesca had a shower
at once, in order to dry her hair in the last hour of sunlight.

Caspar had gone ashore, and had not yet returned as
she sat on the coachroof, catching up thick strands of hair
with a twist of her comb and letting them fan back in
place to speed up the process of drying.

The one slight flaw in her pleasurable anticipation was
the fact that her only pair of sandals were not really right
for her dress. But as she would not be dancing—not
knowing how—her feet would be under the table, and
probably no one would notice that what the dress needed

were gold sandals rather than red ones.

Unconsciously she had been keeping watch for the first glimpse of Caspar's tall figure walking back to their berth. When at length he came into view, it occurred to her to wonder where he had gone. Maybe, as he was carrying a plastic carrier, he had been to buy another bottle of rum for the daiquiris which were their friends' favourite drinks in the evening.

'Hair nearly dry?' he asked, coming onboard with the lightness which never failed to surprise her in anyone of his great height.

'Nearly.'

'Try these for size, Cinderella.' In one smooth action he went down on his haunches beside her and produced what was clearly a shoe-box.

'Caspar!' she gasped, when she saw the expensive evening sandals as he took them from their tissue wrappings.

They were classic T-straps, held in place at the toe by a narrow band of gold kid studded with brilliants. The height of the heels made her wonder if she could walk on them.

'Oh, they're lovely—but what must they have cost? I'm sure you can't really afford them. You shouldn't lavish your money on me,' she exclaimed, in mingled joy and dismay.

'Pretty legs deserve pretty shoes,' he responded lightly, as he slipped the left one on her foot.

Francesca had to check an impulse to lean down and lay her cheek on the dark head bent to the task of fastening the tiny gilt buckle.

'Thank you, Caspar,' she said huskily. 'They're perfect for my new dress. How clever of you to remember the size I take.'

'I checked the size from your red ones. The saleswoman said they would change them if they weren't a good fit, but they seem to be excellent,' he said, as he fastened the other. He straightened. 'Try standing in them.'

She stood up, her insteps arched by the curve of the soles.

'I ought to have painted toenails. Do my unpainted ones look peculiar?'

'They look the way girls' toes should look, and too often don't. Most feet are better concealed, but yours have never been spoiled by being forced into ill-fitting shoes.'

Francesca tried a few steps, turned, wobbled, and clutched at his arms for support.

'You have good natural balance. You'll soon get used to them,' said Caspar, grasping her by the elbows.

'It's amazing how raised-up I feel. If three inches makes all this difference, what must it be like to see the world from your vantage point?'

Even on high heels, she was still inches shorter than he.

Caspar looked down at her, smiling at her excitement. Something in his expression made her feel very young and naïve, and suddenly she wanted to make him understand that she wasn't a child any longer, but a girl on the brink of womanhood. The impulse which she had suppressed on the day he had given her the sewing-machine now rose to the surface again, and would no longer be denied.

Not caring who might be watching, forgetting they were supposed to be brother and sister, she closed the short space between them and, flinging her arms round his neck, pressed a kiss on his cheek, very close to his firm, smiling mouth.

'Darling Caspar ... you are so good to me,' she murmured, deliberately pressing against him with the whole of her slim, towel-wrapped body, and keeping her lips to the dark brown, beard-shadowed skin in the hope of being kissed in return.

For a moment his arms closed round her, locking her to him with a strength which was both exciting and frightening. For years of her life the superior strength of the male had been a thing to be dreaded. Now, for the first time, she experienced it, not in a nightmare merely, but in reality. And even though it was Caspar, whom she knew and trusted, who held her inescapably pinioned in an embrace which she herself had initiated, her instinctive reaction was a surge of resistance.

'You're welcome.'

He pushed her away, not ungently but with a deliberation as unequivocal as that with which she had snuggled against him.

'Watch it—your towel's coming adrift,' he added.

Automatically, her hands flew to her chest to grab the towel before it collapsed. But although it had loosened a little, it was in no danger of collapsing.

'Time I had my shower,' said Caspar, stepping aside to go past her.

When he had disappeared below, Francesca sat down and stuck out her golden-shod feet, and stared unseeingly at the brilliants.

Why hadn't he kissed her? Had she made a fool of herself by tacitly asking to be kissed?

She knew he had not been unmoved by her hug, and her tentative kiss. But perhaps any man in his place, on finding a girl cuddling up to him, would have reacted as he had. His response could have been as involuntary as her instant of fear.

It was a long time since his brief liaison with Beverley Vogt. As far as she knew, he had lived like a monk ever since. Probably, now, any female's embrace would excite him.

Not being without certain scruples, he had pushed her away because it was not her he wanted, and he wasn't the type to take advantage of her inexperience. Maybe it wasn't even a matter of scruple with him; just a prosaic and selfish wish to avoid complications. At the cost of some self-control, he preferred to batten down his urges until the next sex-hungry older woman came into his orbit.

But I could give him so much more than they do. I would give him the whole of love, not just that one part, thought Francesca.

The thought had been in her mind for several minutes before its full significance hit her. Somewhere along the way, at a moment impossible to pinpoint, her liking for Caspar had blossomed.

He was no longer merely her rescuer and protector, but the man she loved and wanted to stay with for ever.

She did not emerge from her cabin until he tapped on the door, and called, 'Are you nearly ready, Francesca? It's time we were leaving.'

'I shan't be more than a minute.'

She heard him moving away, and turned for a final glance at herself in the mirror. The green dress intensified the colour of her eyes, and she was pleased with the success of the hairstyle she had seen in one of Harriet's magazines, and copied. For the first time ever she was wearing lipstick, a colour called Apricot Melba which she had chosen on the advice of the girl behind the cosmetics counter, and paid for with some of her earnings.

Caspar was waiting to lock up when she joined him on deck.

'I approve of the dress,' he said, scrutinising it.

'Thank you.'

Remembering her boldness earlier, Francesca blushed and avoided his eyes. But while he was locking the main hatch, she took stock of him and thought how personable he looked in a shirt she had not seen before, with a tie, and well-cut linen trousers.

Then she remembered his heritage. It was not surprising he looked distinguished. He *was* distinguished.

He turned to hand her ashore, and they walked to where *Sea Spray* was berthed and found the Scott-Leighs drinking champagne with their baby-sitter, Mrs Clive.

'You look stunning, Francesca,' said Harriet, who was herself looking very attractive in a white halter top and a Mexican skirt of black cotton, the two cinched by a cyclamen belt to match her evening sandals. She had cascades of small silver bobbles swinging from her ears, and a jingle of silver bracelets on her left wrist.

'A little present from me, Francesca,' said Sam, handing her a small oblong package. 'I gather it's a special occasion—your début, as it were.'

'How very nice of you. Thank you.' She took off the paper, and gave a murmur of pleasure. 'French scent! Oh, Sam . . .' Words failed her, but her face glowed.

'Worth a kiss?' he asked, offering his cheek.

'Worth a dozen.' She kissed him warmly and unselfconsciously, then turned to press his wife's arm, and say in a low voice, 'And thank *you* for my dress, dearest Harriet. How kind everyone has been. Did you notice my sandals . . . from Caspar?'

Before the evening was over she had not only become accustomed to walking on high heels, but had danced on them.

'Nonsense. Of course you can dance,' Caspar insisted, when at first she refused his suggestion that they follow the other two on to the floor.

As usual, he had been right. After a few minutes of acute selfconsciousness, she had found that she was capable of copying the movements of the other dancers. By the time the music stopped she had begun to enjoy herself.

Sam claimed that he danced only to please his wife, and until the floor-show at midnight they danced every dance together, except for one when Sam partnered Francesca. Caspar stood up for all the lively music, but not for most of the slower numbers. When he did dance one of these with her, he did not hold her close in the manner of all the other couples.

She took this as a clear confirmation that he wanted to

keep their relationship on an impersonal footing.

Out of consideration for Mrs Clive, they did not stay on for more dancing after the floor-show. Their taxi back to the harbour took Mrs Clive home. Having proposed coffee and a nightcap or two on his boat, Sam said, 'Care for a stroll to the end of the sea wall and back while the girls are making the coffee?'

'Yes, why not?' Caspar agreed.

As soon as the two men had set off, Harriet beckoned Francesca to follow her to the galley.

'Sam doesn't really want to stretch his legs,' she said. 'There's something he wants to tell Caspar . . . something he didn't mention earlier in case it blighted our evening out.'

'I—I don't understand,' Francesca said apprehensively.

Her friend went through to the day cabin, returning a few seconds later with an envelope in her hand. It bore British stamps, and from it protruded a letter and a fold of newsprint.

'I wrote to Sam's mother and mentioned that we'd met Caspar,' she said. 'I didn't expect a reply from her, but this came today. She wanted it to catch us before we left here. Caspar's grandfather is dead, which makes him the new Lord Lanyon. She enclosed the old man's obituary from *The Times* of two weeks ago.'

She handed Francesca the newspaper cutting.

The obituary notice was a long one, mentioning all the principal events of the late Marquis's long life from his birth in 1895.

His wife was dismissed in three lines. *He married in 1920 Lady Iris Walsham, youngest daughter of the Duke of Cumberland, by whom he had three sons.*

It then gave the dates of the births and deaths of his sons, the two eldest of whom had died without issue. His third son was stated to have married Miss Doreen Potts of Islington, by whom he had had one son, the late Marquis's heir and successor. The obituary concluded with the instruction to *see Page 3, Col. 5*.

'What was on page three, I wonder?' said Francesca, when she had finished reading the clipping.

Harriet fished in the envelope. 'Mama-in-law sent that, too.' She handed over a second cutting.

This one was of greater interest, for it showed a photograph of a much younger but instantly recognisable Caspar, taken with another young man, both of them having goggles slung round their necks, and the friend wearing a woolly hat.

'Sam recognised that as a snap which he took on a skiing holiday,' Harriet explained, as Francesca looked from the broad grin which Caspar's companion was directing at the camera, to the more restrained lopsided smile of the taller, bare-headed boy with the wind-ruffled black forelock.

The news story with the pictures said that, following the death of his grandfather, world-wide enquiries were being made by the family solicitors to discover the present whereabouts of the ninth Marquis.

He had last been seen as one of the pall-bearers at his grandmother's burial in the family vault, although he had performed this office in the guise of one of the estate workers, being, because of the rift between his father and grandfather, *persona ingrata* at the service in the private chapel at Lanyon.

As Francesca was reading that Caspar had distinguished himself at school by twice being Victor Ludorum, or champion of games, Harriet whisked the cutting out of her hand.

'I can hear the men coming back. Perhaps you shouldn't let on that I showed those to you,' she said, on a conspiratorial note.

There was nothing in Caspar's manner, when he and Sam came aboard, to suggest that he had just received news of a crucial nature. But the next day, after they had

waved goodbye to the party aboard *Sea Spray* as they left
harbour, headed for Antigua, it seemed to her that he did
become unusually preoccupied.

Several times it was on the tip of her tongue to tell him
that she knew what was on his mind; but each time her
nerve failed her in case he was annoyed with her for
knowing something he would have preferred to keep to
himself.

She found it impossible to judge his reaction to finding
himself possessed of an ancient title and a great if decay-
ing house in England. He must always have known that
both would become his some day, except in the unnatural
event of his predeceasing his grandfather.

Next day they set sail for Montserrat, a small island
named after a Spanish monastery and recommended by
the Scott-Leighs who had made it their base the previous
winter. This suggested that Caspar did not intend to take
any immediate action to claim his inheritance.

As day followed day, and Caspar revealed nothing of
his thoughts, Francesca's suspense increased until she
could bear it no longer. One evening, when they were at
anchor off the southern coast of Montserrat, she said,
'Harriet told me about your grandfather. I suppose it
means that you won't be going back to chartering after
all?'

He gave her a long look. 'She shouldn't have told you.
I suppose you've been worrying about what would
happen to you if I went back to England?'

'Worrying?—No,' she said untruthfully. 'I'm much
better equipped to make my own way in the world than I
was when you rescued me, Caspar. Thanks to Emmy
Tate and your sewing machine, I know I can earn my
living now. You can go back to England without any
qualms on my account.'

'I shall take you with me,' was his answer.

Her heart leapt, but only momentarily. 'No, it
wouldn't do,' she said quietly. 'With chartering, I could

have been useful—but not in England. And the climate
there wouldn't suit me. I prefer it here, in the sun.'

'So do I, but I have to go back; and where I go, you
go, *chiquilla*. You may have come of age legally, but that
doesn't make you grown-up in my definition of the term.
You can bring the sewing machine with you, and make
tea-cosies instead of beach bags. No, don't argue with me.
I'm going to have problems enough without worrying
what's happening to you.'

'But I'm not your responsibility, Caspar. It's absurd to
add me to your burdens.'

'Keeping an eye on you will be the least of them. I've
got used to having you around. You're no trouble—when
you do as you're told. Now go and attend to my supper,
there's a good girl.'

He gave her a push with one hand, and a friendly
spank with the other.

Half that night Francesca lay awake, torn between her
longing to go with him, and her feeling that he couldn't
really want her, but felt it was his duty to take her.

In the early hours of the morning, when she had not
been sleeping for long, she woke up to find they were
under way. After pulling on jeans and a banana-coloured
velours top bequeathed her by Harriet who had decided
that the colour didn't suit her, she went on deck.

Caspar was at the helm. In the moonlight his strong,
rawboned features might have been hewn out of teak.

The wind was abaft the beam; a fresh breeze that filled
Rain's sails and swept her across the light swell at a good
seven knots, foaming white wings at her bows and a long
train of white froth astern.

'Is this our last night at sea?' she asked him, after a
while.

'I'm afraid so—at least for some time. I don't want to
leave the islands any more than you do, but the motto of
my family is *Semper*, which is Latin for Always, and I find
now that my turn has come that it's not so easy to turn

my back on it all. Although God knows I've never wanted any of it,' he added sombrely. 'How much did Harriet tell you?'

'Only that both your uncles were killed as young men, and there was an estrangement between your father and grandfather. Is your mother alive?'

'No.'

Even if she had known nothing about his parents, the expressionless negative would have suggested that his relationship with his mother had not been a close one. Perhaps she had killed something in him; making it impossible for him to feel anything for women but the sexual desire aroused by Beverley Vogt, or the brotherly kindness which was all she herself seemed to inspire in him.

CHAPTER SIX

THREE days later she had her first experience of air travel. For much of the flight Caspar slept, but Francesca was far too strung up with nervous excitement to be capable even of dozing.

They had been advised by a travel agent that a good place to spend their night in London would be the Selfridge Hotel beside the great store of the same name. It was also near Marks & Spencer, said Caspar, where, on their first morning in England, she would be able to equip herself with inexpensive but good quality warm clothes while he went to see his solicitors in the City, the central and most ancient part of London to the east of the fashionable shopping streets of the West End.

The flight took nearly nine hours, but seemed longer in spite of an in-flight film and several meals to break the monotony of sitting still for so long. However, because of

the time-change, by the clock it was more than twelve
hours after their departure from Antigua when at last
they landed at Heathrow, there to wait, with passengers
from several other incoming flights, for the two big suit-
cases to appear on one of the conveyors.

Had she been on her own, Francesca would have been
bewildered by the crowd of people of many different
nationalities who were milling about in the baggage hall.
She would not have known that luggage trolleys were
available, or on which of the several conveyors their baggage would eventually appear.

However, having flown to Switzerland and other parts
of Europe during his schooldays, Caspar knew the drill
and was soon in possession of a trolley, after which he
relaxed until the number of their flight appeared on one
of the signs above each conveyor.

Even so they were not among the first to pass through
into the Customs Hall. Having retrieved their belongings,
he delayed to help a pair of elderly women who were
burdened with large, heavy cases which required the
strength of a man to heave them off the conveyor.

Watching them, Francesca saw their perturbed faces
relax into grateful relief. No one else seemed to have
noticed their concern, or perhaps others had noticed it
but lacked Caspar's innate chivalry towards anyone in a
difficulty which he had the power to relieve. The only
time she had known him to withhold his help was when,
long ago, she had begged him to give her and her father a
passage to the coast. Even then he had changed his mind
later, and turned back up-river to fetch them.

Although they had nothing to declare, a Customs officer made a swift search of the cases which contained all
the personal possessions Casper had not wished to leave
on *Rain*.

Soon afterwards, Francesca found herself in a coach
which took them to the terminal at Victoria where they
transferred to a taxi. This final phase of the journey had

her perched on the edge of the seat, her eyes bright with renewed excitement as Caspar pointed out a high wall with spikes on top which he said surrounded the Queen's garden. A few minutes later he directed her attention to a tall old mansion, standing on the corner of Hyde Park, which he told her was Apsley House, the home of the first Duke of Wellington and, during his lifetime, the scene of the annual Waterloo banquet.

'Is it something like Lanyon?' she asked, peering out of his side of the taxi at the impressive columned façade.

'Lanyon is larger.'

'Larger!' Francesca ejaculated.

Apsley House looked enormous to her. Lanyon must be the size of a palace.

They began to speed up Park Lane, with the trees of the dark park on one side, and towering hotels on the other. She had a brief glimpse of the stores and shops lining Oxford Street, and then they were at their destination, and a liveried doorman was helping her out of the taxi while one of the hotel baggage porters attended to their luggage and Caspar paid off the driver.

The interior of the hotel was quite different from any of those she had entered in the Caribbean. Everywhere was thickly carpeted and panelled with dark glossy wood. It was also comfortably warm, but with a different kind of warmth from that to which she was accustomed.

At the reception desk, Caspar was given a form to fill in. Standing beside him, Francesca noticed that he wrote *C. Brown and Miss Brown*, in care of the address of his bank.

Their rooms were next door to each other. Having been used for so long to the confined spaces of a boat, hers seemed very large to her.

'When you've washed, come next door and we'll order some sandwiches and coffee from Room Service,' he said, after glancing into her room and before moving on to the next one.

All her overnight requirements were in her canvas shoulder bag. The bed had already been turned down. She unpacked her sleeping cloth and placed it on the pillow. Then she took out her toilet bag and went to the adjoining bathroom, which was almost as large as her sleeping cabin on the sloop.

She found it difficult to grasp that, between waking and sleeping, she had spanned the Atlantic and was now in a different world where many things were unfamiliar.

Under Caspar's protective aegis, this new world could hold no terrors. But had she arrived here without him, how would she have managed? she wondered, as she washed her hands.

When he opened his door in response to her knock, she found him in his shirt-sleeves with the window flung wide.

'I find it hard to adjust to the stuffiness of closed windows and central heating; but, if you feel chilly, I'll close it,' he said, seeing the direction of her glance.

'No, it is rather close, I agree. But better than shivering,' she added. 'Caspar, why did you give us false names when you signed the register?'

'Are you worried about it?' he asked her, with an intent look.

'No—nothing you did would worry me. I was puzzled, that's all.'

'I don't want the Press getting wind of my arrival, as they might if I'd registered under my real name. It's not illegal to use a false name providing one does it merely to protect one's privacy and not with criminal intent.'

'What is your real name now?' she asked. 'What would you have written, had you not been incognito?'

'Just Lanyon. The address I gave was in case we should happen to leave anything behind here. I hope you won't find yourself shivering at Lanyon, this time to-morrow. If the place is too much like a tomb, we shall have to put up at the pub. But after tonight it won't do to continue to pose as brother and sister. It's well known that I have no sister. We shall have to find some other way to account for our association.'

The floor waiter arrived with a trolley on which, in addition to sandwiches and a pot of coffee, there was a bottle of champagne in a silver bucket full of ice.

When they were once more on their own, Caspar said, 'This will help you to sleep on your first night ashore for a long time.'

He handed her one of the glasses filled by the waiter.

Francesca said, 'The last night I spent ashore was in that dreadful hotel where Father and I were living when we met you. It seems a lifetime ago.'

'Yes, you've changed a great deal since those days,' he said, eyeing her thoughtfully. 'But not as much as you'll change from now on, I daresay.'

'Why shall I change from now on?'

But Caspar chose not to enlighten her. Instead he offered her a sandwich, and said he must call the Scott-Leighs. And Francesca had long since learned better than to attempt to press him on a subject he had decided to drop, even though it was he who had raised it.

She listened to his chat with Sam, and herself had a brief talk with Harriet, who was vexed that they were not putting up with her for the night.

The following morning, before leaving Francesca to her own devices, Caspar marched her to the nearest shoe shop to supervise the buying of a pair of serviceable walking shoes.

'I know what women are. If I leave the choice to you, you will probably succumb to something fashionable rather than practical,' he said crushingly, in response to her protest that she was capable of undertaking this purchase on her own. 'We're going to be doing a great deal of tramping about in the next week or two. You'll only be an encumbrance if you aren't properly shod.'

Uneasily conscious of being an encumbrance to him whether sensibly-shod or otherwise, she subsided into passive submission.

The stout leather shoes wrapped and paid for, Caspar then said he would accompany her to the famous chain store, to help her to buy the basics of her English wardrobe.

'After which I'll leave you to choose the rest as you think fit. Just bear in mind that, unless it's been modernised, which Lanyon hasn't, there's nowhere colder and draughtier than a large English country house. There'll be many days this summer when you'll feel very chilly,' he warned her. 'We're lucky, we've arrived in an early heatwave. But it isn't always like this.'

Caspar's idea of a basic wardrobe was a raincoat, a pleated tweed skirt, a pair of needlecord pants and a couple of snug wool sweaters.

'Now I must get off to my appointment,' he said, with a glance at his watch. 'If you don't spend the money I've given you, I shall bring you back later and make you. But it would be much more convenient to set out for Lanyon immediately after lunch. So be a good girl and do as you're told. See you later.'

With a casual pat on the shoulder, he strode off towards the nearest exit, leaving Francesca to wonder if he could really afford what, to her seemed a great deal of money.

At present the notes were in a cotton zip-purse on a long cord which she had made for herself. On the telephone the night before, Harriet had agreed that at Marks and Sparks, as she called it, Francesca would be able to buy almost everything she needed. But when it came to buying a bag, Harriet had recommended the vast department store next door, and also for cosmetics, because they had all the best brands, often at special offer prices.

Thus, having taken her first handful of bright green carriers back to the hotel, and left them in the care of the

baggage porter who already had their cases in his charge,
she ventured into the huge store and wended her way
through all the fascinating departments on the ground
floor until she came to the bags, where there was such a
large selection it was hard to know what to choose.

Always, whenever the chance had come her way, she
had enjoyed looking round shops. But that first morning
in London, on her own, with more money safely bestowed
in the centre compartment of her new leather bag than
she had ever dreamed of having to spend, she discovered
that buying was even better than window-gazing.

Far from feeling alone and bereft in an alien environ-
ment, she could have been happy to spend the whole day
looking, comparing and selecting. However, as Caspar
had told her to meet him for lunch at one o'clock in the
hotel's Picnic Basket restaurant, she had to keep an eye
on the time.

It was ten minutes to one when she returned to the
hotel to be given a message from Caspar. He had been
delayed. She was to have lunch by herself. He would
collect her at half past two, having had lunch himself in
the meantime.

It would have suited her better to have a sandwich and
a cup of coffee in the lounge. But she felt he might take
her to task if he found she had had only a snack. So she
went to the Picnic Basket, which seemed to be patronised
mainly by women and overseas tourists. A table for two
was drawn out for her, so that she could sit on the banquette and discreetly observe her fellow lunchers.

Waiting for her cottage cheese salad and a glass of
grapefruit juice to be brought, she noticed how pale were
all these European faces compared with the suntanned
and naturally dark-skinned complexions of the people
she was accustomed to seeing. She looked with interest
at the details of the women's clothes. Some were very
well dressed, but others seemed lacking in some way, and
she found it interesting to try to analyse the difference

between elegance and inelegance.

When Caspar returned he was driving a small hired car.

'Lanyon used to have its own railway station on one of the scores of small branch lines which ran all over the Home Counties,' he told her, as they crossed the Thames. 'But those small lines were closed years ago.'

The broad expanse of the river shimmered in the sun, but it wasn't blue like the Caribbean, nor could Francesca see any sailing vessels, only barges and launches and a dredger. She wondered if Caspar, too, was feeling a pang of regret for the carefree life left behind.

The route out of London was through miles of indistinguishable suburbs, all rather seedy. She saw many West Indian faces and wondered if they pined for their islands. For her, anywhere with Caspar was preferable to parting from him.

The ugliness of outer London had not prepared her for the beauty of the open countryside beyond the sprawl of the city. As they turned off main roads on to minor roads, driving sometimes down narrow lanes where field-gates gave glimpses of farms surrounded by old barns, or the ivy-clad ruin of an abbey, she began to realise that perhaps this was not, after all, so poor an exchange for the happy months aboard *Rain*.

Sometimes braking to check his road map, Caspar followed a route which took them past ancient mills and through villages of tile-hung cottages built around greens, some with ponds. Everywhere there were old parish churches, some with lychgates and some with arches of dark close-clipped yew above the entrance to the churchyards where daffodils nodded in the grass between the leaning gravestones.

At last, coming to a crossroads where a high brick wall bordered one side of the lane ahead and also the lane to their right, Caspar said, 'Not far now. That's the north and east boundary of Lanyon.'

But it was a mile, if not more, before the high wall was broken by a splendid entrance. It was formed of a pediment supported by two pairs of columns with screens of wrought iron between them, and a great pair of gates in the central space. These were chained and padlocked when Caspar braked and climbed out to walk towards them. However, as he approached from the outside, an old man appeared on the inside. He must have been waiting in the porch of the lodge house inside the gates, although the lodge itself had a shuttered, deserted appearance.

From her seat in the car, Francesca could not hear the first words he and Caspar exchanged. Presently, when the younger man had helped the old one to pull the massive gates inwards, he came back to the car and drove it through them.

Then he stopped a few yards inside and assisted the old man to close them again.

'This is Piper, my grandfather's valet, Francesca. I met Miss Hartley's father in South America where unfortunately he died, leaving her in my care,' explained Caspar, before he tipped forward the driving seat to allow the aged retainer—he appeared to be at least seventy-five —to climb slowly and stiffly into the back of the small car.

'Good afternoon, miss,' he said to her.

She gave him a shy smile. 'Good afternoon.'

Caspar climbed in, started the car and began an erratic progress up a long, tree-lined drive in such a bad state of repair that he was continually swerving to avoid the worst ruts and pot-holes.

'Are all the estate roads as bad as this, Piper?' he asked, over his shoulder.

'The road from the West Gate is the only one kept up now, m'lord. You should have been told that this road was no longer in use. But although we were warned to expect you very soon now, Mrs Bray became somewhat flustered when she heard your lordship's voice on the telephone this morning. Had I been in the house at the time, I should have advised you to arrive by way of the West Gate.'

'It makes no odds to us, Piper, but it would have saved you the long walk to open the main gates. How long have they been locked?'

'Since old Mr Piggott was taken away to a Home, which is six years ago at Easter, m'lord. He is still alive, but quite senile. Mrs Bray went to see him on his ninety-fourth birthday, but he didn't recognise her.'

'This is an old man who began as a gardener's boy in my great-grandfather's time,' Caspar explained to Francesca. 'He worked his way up to head gardener. He and his wife lived at the Lodge, and Mrs Piggott opened and shut the gates which, being in good order at that time, weren't difficult for her to handle. Mrs Bray was my grandmother's maid,' he added.

Presently she began to understand his remark about a long walk. The drive seemed to go on for miles, winding its way through acres of parkland and woodland until at last, from the crest of a rise, they saw the great house in its sheltered, south-facing hollow, with the lake beyond it gleaming in the spring sunlight.

Caspar had already told her that Lanyon, designed in 1721, had taken twenty years to build, and ranked as a leading example of the English Palladian style of architecture.

But he had not prepared her for the grandeur of the North Front with its golden sandstone façade and balustraded roof surmounted with lidded stone urns. Palatial as was the main block, it was flanked by two lower wings—each the size of a large country house—linked to it by colonnades.

Seeing Lanyon spread out before her for the first time, Francesca could not repress a smothered gasp of wonder that so much magnificence was his. It brought home to

her, more than before, the great gulf which now yawned
between them.

Had she grown up in England, even if she had never
actually set foot in any of the many stately homes open to
the public, she would have been sure to have seen pictures of them, or glimpses on television. But growing up
as she had in Central and South America, and sharing
the steady decline of her father's fortunes, her introduction to Lanyon had an overpoweringly strong effect on
her.

As they entered the house by way of its famous
Painted Hall, she was not aware of the dust which lay
thickly on the stonework of the lower storey, below the
murals, or the threadbare state of the carpet on the staircase, as wide as the drive, which ascended to the first
floor. She saw none of the signs of neglect, but only a
splendour and beauty beyond her wildest imaginings.

Pilasters of Derbyshire alabaster rising up to a ceiling
depicting a goddess and her nymphs, pedestals supporting
white marble busts of history's greatest men, and a floor
of multi-coloured marble made her green eyes widen in
wonder.

Their arrival must have been watched for. A number of elderly persons were lined up to greet the new
Marquis.

Francesca stood on one side, feeling very much an outsider, while Piper presented these people to Caspar. There
were only two women among them; a cook, and the
former lady's maid whom, presently, Caspar in turn introduced to her, saying, 'Mrs Bray, would you take Miss
Hartley to whichever room has been prepared for her?
She's a stranger to England, and has had a long, tiring
journey. I'm sure I can rely on you to make her welcome,
and as comfortable as possible.'

'With pleasure, m'lord. Would you like to come this
way, Miss Hartley?' Mrs Bray smiled, and gestured towards the great staircase.

She was somewhat younger than her male colleagues,

perhaps not much more than sixty. She had curly grey hair, and her neat dress was also dark grey, with a cameo brooch at the neck.

At the top of the stairs, she turned left down a long corridor hung with tapestries on one side and oil paintings on the other. Chairs, tables and sofas were arranged in the spaces between, and the floor was laid with many rugs.

'This is called the Small Gallery,' explained Mrs Bray. 'We've put you in Her Ladyship's dressing-room where I used to sleep when she was ill. It's easier to heat than her bedroom and we thought you would feel the cold, coming from a much warmer climate. But if it's too small, we can move you elsewhere. The rooms used by guests in the old days are very damp now. His Lordship will have a hard task to put things right, I'm afraid.'

'I understand you were with Lord Lanyon's grandmother for a long time?' said Francesca hesitantly.

'All my working life, except for a few months. Lady Lanyon had a French maid before me, but she didn't like her. I came here from my first post as a young ladies' maid, and I stayed here until I was married in 1939. My husband and young Lord Newark were both killed in 1940, so I came back to Lanyon, and here I've been ever since.'

The small Gallery led to a landing at the head of another great staircase from which a narrower corridor led to the late Marchioness's boudoir. Here the tall windows overlooked a rose garden, and a distant view of a temple on the fringe of a wood.

Adjoining the boudoir was the dressing-room, much larger than Francesca had imagined, with a single bed tucked in a corner between two mahogany wardrobes, and a wallpaper patterned with white bamboos on a blue ground. Off this was an equally large bathroom, the bath encased in mahogany with three shining brass taps, one marked *Rain*.

'You'll find the water nice and hot, and this part of the

house has electric light, which the State Rooms haven't,'
said Mrs Bray. 'Her Ladyship liked to be comfortable,
but after her death His Lordship became very difficult.
He wouldn't spend a penny on anything. But that's in the
past. We hope for better things now.'

While they were talking Francesca's luggage was
brought up by a man whom, when he had gone, Mrs
Bray described as 'a little moonstruck, but he makes himself useful.'

Shortly afterwards the cook, known as Amy, brought a
tray of tea. She seemed disposed to stay and chat, but
with considerable tact Mrs Bray sent her back to her own
domain.

'She's a good soul, and we can't afford to lose her, but
she's not one of the old school. She doesn't know her
place, Miss Hartley,' she said apologetically.

Nor do I, Francesca thought wryly. Is there a place
here for me?

While she had tea and toast and seedcake, Mrs Bray unpacked her belongings. If she shared the cook's curiosity
about the new Marquis's unexpected companion, she was
far too well trained to indulge it.

Presently she said, 'You do look very tired, Miss Hartley. Why not have a nap on the chaise-longue?'

'I feel sleepy,' Francesca admitted. 'It's not a bit like
me. I suppose it's the long flight yesterday, and the
excitement of shopping this morning.'

'London shops are very exhausting if you're not accustomed to them.'

Mrs Bray proceeded to make her comfortable with a
pile of cushions at her back, a light blanket over her legs
and a hot water bottle at her feet.

When Francesca awoke it was no longer daylight. The
curtains had been drawn across the tall window, and the
room was lit by one table-lamp. Not knowing what time
it grew dark in England, but sensing that she had slept for

much longer than she intended, she looked about her for
a clock. According to the one on the chest of drawers it
was nine o'clock, but perhaps the clock was not going.
She had flung off the blanket and was about to cross the
room to see if it was ticking when the door opened and
Mrs Bray entered.

'Ah, you're awake, Miss Hartley. I've looked in once
or twice, but you were sleeping so soundly that I hesitated to wake you, and when I consulted His Lordship
he said you shouldn't be disturbed. We thought you
might sleep through the night but, if not, he gave instructions that you were to have supper in bed, and he would
see you at breakfast.'

'Oh . . . I see. He's had dinner by now, I suppose?'

'Yes, he dined at eight. I believe he intends to have an
early night himself. Amy has gone back to the village.
She doesn't live in. She has an invalid father who requires
her attention at night. His Lordship had soup and cold
roast beef with salad for dinner, but I should be pleased
to make an omelette for you. It might be more digestible
at this hour.'

'Thank you, Mrs Bray. It's very kind of you, but I
have a cast-iron digestion, and the cold roast beef will be
fine.'

After her solitary supper, Francesca had a long bath.
Mrs Bray would have run it for her, and lingered until
she was in bed. But even if she had been accustomed
to being waited on, Francesca would not have felt comfortable at keeping from leisure a woman of Mrs Bray's
age.

By the time she had dried, and cleaned the bath with
some scouring paste found in a cupboard beneath it, it
was a quarter past ten. No longer tired, she needed
something to read, but the dressing-room offered no
books.

Thinking there might be something, if only a Bible, in
the Marchioness's bedroom next door, she put on her new

long nightdress of green and white voile, and a housecoat
of emerald velours, and ventured into the next room.

It did not take her long to locate a panel of light
switches, and to press all four of them downwards. The
result was a flood of subdued peachy light cast by two
wall lamps and two table-lamps.

The bedroom thus softly illuminated was a large and
lofty apartment dominated by a Venetian window hung
with the same apricot silk which covered the walls. The
bed was a gilded four-poster hung with white silk taffeta
draperies bound with a sky-blue ribbon which repeated a
colour found in the apricot and topaz carpet.

But what caught her eye as much as the room's fine
proportions and elegant furnishings were all the personal
knick-knacks assembled by its last occupant. On a table
not far from the door was a collection of tiny animals
carved from coloured stones, the only one which she recognised being jade. Francesca picked them up one by
one. A two-inch-tall rabbit with red eyes. Could they be
rubies? A black sea lion on an ice floe which must be
crystal. A blue mouse. A grey-green snail.

'My grandmother collected little objects by Fabergé.
Do you like them?'

Francesca jumped and swung round. She had not
heard Caspar enter by a door on the far side of the room.
She was pleased to see him, but at the same time embarrassed at being found in a room where perhaps she ought
not to be.

'Yes, they're beautifully carved. I-I wasn't prying,' she
said hastily. 'I came in to look for a book. Having slept
for a long time earlier, I don't feel like sleeping just yet.'

He came towards her, his hands thrust into the pockets
of a very dark red silk dressing-gown worn over pale grey
pyjamas which she hadn't known he possessed, unless he
had bought them that day.

'My dear girl, explore where you please. I haven't
been in here before. I only recognised those objects be-

cause my grandmother spoke of them, and I've seen one or two in museums. Are you happy with where you're sleeping? Not nervous of being on your own?'

'Oh, no, my room is quite cosy. Have a look,' she suggested, indicating the door.

He went to the threshold and briefly inspected her quarters.

'Better than mine,' he said dryly. 'They've put me in the old boy's room which is as cold as a crypt, and equally gloomy.'

'Can't you move? Must you stay there?' she asked.

'I'll stay there tonight, as the bed's aired. Tomorrow I'll choose somewhere else. There's no shortage of bedrooms—there must be twenty at least. In the morning I'll show you the Library, but it will be too cold tonight. There are some books in the Cabinet where I sat after dinner. I'll take you there now,' he invited.

It would have been eerie on her own in the great silent house, with the staff quarters far away. Escorted by Caspar, she could look about her with interest and no unease.

The embers of a fire were still burning behind a spark screen in the room he had called the Cabinet. Francesca chose two books from a bookcase, and wished he would stoke up the fire and talk to her for a while about the problems which faced him. But although the room was still warm, he showed no inclination to linger.

Going back up the stairs, she caught her toe in a threadbare patch of the carpet and would have stumbled had not Caspar seized her arm.

'That's a death-trap,' he said, seeing the worn place. And then, noticing that her feet were bare, 'Didn't you buy any slippers this morning?'

'No, I should have, but I forgot—not being used to wearing them. It doesn't matter. My feet aren't cold.'

'Perhaps not, but there may be splinters where the floor upstairs isn't carpeted.'

Before she realised what he meant to do, he had swung her up in his arms, one strong arm under her knees and the other cradling her back.

'Put your arm round my neck,' he instructed.

It seemed a much shorter distance back to her room than it had on the way to the Cabinet. She found herself thinking how much nicer it would be if, instead of sleeping in his grandfather's large, gloomy bedroom, he could stay with her in the dressing-room. Her bed there was only a single one, but with enough room for two people if they lay very close. What bliss it would be to sleep and wake on his shoulder, to receive her first kiss from his lips, and learn about love in his arms.

The train of her thoughts made her shiver and, thinking her chilled, Caspar said, 'This green velvet thing is becoming, but I think wool would have been warmer.'

They came to the dressing-room where she thought he would set her on her feet. Instead he waited for her to open the door. Inside, he shouldered it shut.

Still holding her close to his chest, he crossed to the bed and lowered her on to it.

As her hand slid away from his neck, she took hold of the collar of his dressing-gown.

'Caspar, don't go for a moment. I want to tell you h-how grateful I am for being brought here. I don't know how I can make myself useful, but there must be some way I can repay all your kindness.'

Her grasp on the rolled silk collar achieved the result she had wanted. He sat down on the edge of the bed, a frown contracting his eyebrows as he studied her faintly flushed face.

'It's a pity you're not five years younger . . . or five years older,' he said. 'I'm going to have breakfast at seven, then go for a tramp in the woods. You can join me or not, as you wish. Goodnight, Francesca. Sleep well.'

He rose and returned to his room by way of the Marchioness's bedroom, leaving her to wonder if he knew what had been in her mind and would not, had she been some years older, have gone back to his grandfather's bed.

CHAPTER SEVEN

THE grass was silvered with dew, and the air had a fresh, earthy tang when they set out together next morning in the direction of the Tuscan Temple on the edge of the forest of beeches known as the Home Wood.

Soon the air lost its early chill, and the sky held the promise of being as cloudless as yesterday.

To walk among trees without any fear of fierce animals or poisonous snakes was a new experience for Francesca, and she hoped they would walk every morning. If she had only a little of Caspar's time it would be enough for her.

While she was gathering jonquils among the trees, she heard a sound which she did not immediately recognise as the snort of a horse. As she straightened and look around her to see what it might be, she was just in time to see horse and rider come into view from behind a thicket of bushes where the ride along which they were moving was joined by another.

The horse was black; its rider a girl with fair hair. When she caught sight of Caspar strolling towards her, she reined in her mount and, after a short hesitation, swung herself out of the saddle.

She was unusually tall, but neither Amazonian nor gangling. She had an excellent figure displayed to advantage by a pair of fawn jodhpurs and a thick white polo-necked sweater.

As she led her horse up to Caspar, who had stopped

walking as she dismounted, it passed through Francesca's
mind that here was his physical counterpart. The rider
must dwarf most men, but with him her height appeared
normal. Together they looked like two members of a
superior species.

'Good morning. You must be Lord Lanyon, and I,
need I say, am a trespasser.'

The girl's light voice carried clearly to where Francesca was watching her introduce herself.

'Good morning. You're right, I am Lanyon. But you
have nothing to worry about. I'm granting an amnesty to
trespassers—providing they're of your sex, and young and
good-looking,' was his answer.

Francesca's heart sank. In just that particular tone had
Caspar begun his amour with Beverley Vogt.

'Nothing to worry about on *that* score,' said the young
woman, showing her dimples. 'I'm Alethea Spencer. We
used to live at Mallington, but the Carters have it now.
But perhaps the name means nothing to you, as you're
only just back from abroad.'

The reins, which had been in her right hand, she
passed behind her to her left hand, in order to offer the
other to Caspar.

He said, 'On the contrary, I believe my grandmother
and yours were close friends, Miss Spencer. I seem to
recall meeting your grandmother once, when I was a
small boy having tea with mine in London.' Still holding
her hand, he went on, 'The name Carter *is* unknown to
me. You say they have Mallington Hall now?'

She was a self-possessed girl, not at all discomposed by
having her hand held for longer than was strictly necessary.

'Yes, we had to sell it and move to the Dower House
with Granny. She's dead now, and there's more than
enough room there for my parents and me, except that
there's nowhere to ride. So now I come here—or did, in
your grandfather's time.'

'And will continue to do so in my time, I hope.'

'That's very kind of you, but you may want to ride here yourself.'

'I don't ride and, if I did, there's room for more than one person to ride, don't you think?'

'Oh, yes—room for a dozen,' she agreed. 'But even so you might prefer to have it all to yourself. I should, in your place. To be frank, I have to admit I'm the only person who hasn't been eagerly looking forward to your arrival. But that's partly because I thought you might turn out to be as crusty as your grandfather.'

'As I may be in later life, but not yet, I hope.' Caspar let go of her hand and looked over his shoulder. 'Francesca, come and meet one of our neighbours.'

As she returned to the ride with her armful of jonquils, Francesca could not be sure, but she thought she saw in Alethea Spencer's blue eyes a fleeting expression of displeased surprise at finding she was not alone with the old Marquis's amiable successor.

'Francesca Hartley . . . Alethea Spencer,' was Caspar's succinct introduction, as she drew near them.

As they shook hands, he added pleasantly, 'I believe I'm right in saying that, compared with Miss Spencer's family, the Barringtons are mere upstarts.'

'Yes, there aren't very many families who can prove their descent back to Domesday, but there was a Spencer at Mallington in 1086,' she agreed. 'Unfortunately I've spoiled that record.'

'You have no brothers?' asked Caspar.

She shook her head, and something in the gesture made Francesca feel a flash of compassion for her. In this world of old landed families she was an outsider, but it didn't prevent her from sensing that it would be an exceptional father who would never show his disappointment at having no son to continue a line unbroken for nine hundred years.

What with being a girl, and such an exceptionally tall

one, clearly Alethea had had to contend with two sizeable disadvantages in life.

Although his remark had sketched in something of Alethea's background, Caspar did not volunteer any clues concerning Francesca's presence with him. He turned his attention to the horse, running his hand over its neck and not dodging nervously back, as Francesca felt she would have done, when it suddenly tossed up its head.

'You said you didn't ride,' said Alethea. 'Did you mean you can't ride at present because the stables at Lanyon are empty? Or because you don't ride at all?'

'The latter. I'm a helmsman, not a horseman.'

'Oh, you sail? That's great fun, of course, but I think you'll find it a drawback not to ride now you're living at Lanyon. A Land Rover is very useful for getting about an estate, but it has to go round woods, not through them, except by the rides. I have a bay gelding I should be happy to lend you, if you like?'

'Thank you, but I think not. As you say, I may find it necessary to take to horseback, but not for the time being. Shouldn't you be wearing a hard hat when you're riding alone in these woods?'

'Strictly speaking, yes. But I don't—except when I'm hunting, of course. Do you ride, Miss Hartley?'

'No, I don't,' Francesca replied. 'You've ridden from childhood, I expect?'

'Oh, yes. I was put on a pony before I could walk; but it's not impossible for people who take it up later to learn to ride really quite well.'

She continued to chat for some minutes, and then remounted and rode off.

'I have the impression that young woman regards anyone who doesn't ride as being regrettably lacking in one of the most vital attributes,' remarked Caspar dryly, when she had passed out of earshot.

But in spite of his derisive tone, Francesca was not much comforted. She had seen the predatory gleam with which he had watched Miss Spencer raise one booted foot to the stirrup, the movements of mounting drawing attention to her Junoesque hips and thighs.

Later, at lunch, he asked Piper, 'What sort of people are the Carters who live at Mallington Hall now?'

'I believe Mr Carter is not too popular, m'lord. Most people seem to speak more highly of Miss Carter. I can't vouch for the truth of the tale, but it's said that Mr Carter put it about that he would make an offer for Lanyon if the enquiries into Your Lordship's whereabouts proved unsuccessful.'

'Did he indeed? He must be a rich man,' said Caspar.

'A millionaire several times over, so they say, m'lord.'

'Perhaps I should make an offer for Miss Carter,' Caspar said jokingly. 'Is she young? Is she pretty?'

'I believe she is neither, m'lord. Mrs Bray has met her. She could describe Miss Carter to you.'

Caspar laughed. 'Lanyon wouldn't be the first place to be saved from dereliction by a marriage with an unprepossessing heiress. However, it's a measure I don't think I need consider yet. I must admit an alliance with the Magnificent Seven would be more to my taste than an alliance with the rich Miss Carter.'

'Who are the Magnificent Seven?' asked Francesca, when Piper had withdrawn, leaving them to enjoy the roast chicken served with mangetout peas and watercress salad which followed the spinach soup.

'It's the name of a famous film which Tavistock thought of adopting for a publicity alliance between his place, Woburn Abbey, and six other great English houses. About thirty years ago, Tavistock's father, the Duke of Bedford, had to pay five and a half million pounds in death duties. He saved Woburn and most of its treasure by turning it into what some of its stuffier fellow landowners considered an undignified fun-fair. He installed an amusement park and a dolphinarium. People willing to pay for the pleasure of hobnobbing with a duke could dine at the Abbey with him and the Duchess. His ideas caught on. Now Longleat has lions and the world's largest maze, Blenheim has a steam railway and a Churchill exhibition, and Castle Howard has its costume galleries.'

'Are you thinking of doing something similar here?' asked Francesca.

'I don't know yet. It may not be possible. Lanyon may go the way of Mentmore, a great house built by de Rothschild, which went under the hammer in '77. However, a more pressing problem is how to regularise *your* position in my ménage.'

'What do you mean?' she asked uncertainly.

'We can continue with the fiction that your father and I were friends, and he left you under my aegis, but I think there'll still be eyebrows raised in some quarters if we live here together without an older woman to make the arrangement acceptable even in the eyes of the strait-laced.'

'Mrs Bray is an older woman.'

'Yes, but she doesn't count. What we need is a female relation of unmistakable probity. When Piper comes back I'll ask him if he can think of somebody suitable.'

Having pondered Caspar's enquiry while serving the pudding, the old valet who, since the death of his senior colleague, had acted as butler to the late Marquis, and as footman as well since the last one had given his notice, said, 'There is Lady Alice, Your Lordship's great-aunt.'

'I wasn't aware that I had one. You mean my grandfather had a sister? How is it that I've never heard of her?'

'If I may use the expression, she was in disgrace with the late Marquis,' Piper explained. 'Her name was never mentioned, and it was only because Mrs Bray was in Her Ladyship's confidence that we knew Lady Alice to be the person she claimed to be when she came to His Lordship's funeral. Otherwise we should have thought she was an eccentric person who had invented the relationship.'

'How old is she, Piper, and how active?'

'Very active indeed, I should say, m'lord. She must be at least eighty-four, but one wouldn't think so, judging by her appearance. She attended the funeral not out of respect for His Lordship, but from a wish to revisit her childhood home once more. She made herself known to Mrs Bray and myself, and she had the kindness to tell us that, should we find ourselves in difficulties because of the uncertainty about Your Lordship being alive and well, she would be pleased to assist us.'

'So you know where she lives? Far from here?'

'About an hour's journey by motor, m'lord.'

'Right—we'll pay a call on my great-aunt, and if we like her and she likes us, we'll see if she can be persuaded to come and live in her old home,' said Caspar decisively.

Having finished his pudding, he folded his white damask napkin, rolled it and thrust it through a silver ring engraved with the crest of his family's coat of arms.

'No coffee for us today, Piper. Come on, Francesca. Run and fetch your mac—it looks as if it might rain later—while Piper writes down the address, and then we'll be off.'

It was still early afternoon, and the rain clouds had blown away south, when Caspar switched off the engine outside the first cottage in a thatch-roofed, pink-washed row of them. They knew by the name on the gate, *End Cottage*, that this was the one owned by his great-aunt.

With Francesca standing beside him on the path of herringboned brick, Caspar rapped the knocker and waited.

After so long an interval that they thought the old lady must be out, or possibly asleep, the front door suddenly opened and they were confronted by Lady Alice Barrington.

She was wearing what, later, Francesca learned was a slop worn by fishermen. This loose over-garment, of dark blue cotton, was much splashed with paint. Beneath it she had on a sweater and corduroy trousers. The prune-like texture of her complexion, and the corded and freckled state of her hands, betrayed her great age, but her blue eyes were still sharp and shrewd. On her head was a mop of curly synthetic beige hair.

'Good afternoon,' Caspar began.

'Come in, Lanyon,' she said, stepping back. 'Who is this? Your young woman? Your wife?'

'This is Francesca Hartley. You could call her my ward,' he replied.

'Hmph! Quite extraordinary,' said Lady Alice. 'A man of your age in charge of a pretty young girl? Most unsuitable, I should have thought. How d'you do, Miss Hartley. Come in.'

Probably the interior of the cottage had originally consisted of two small rooms and a scullery. It was now all one room with a kitchen area at the rear, and the rest arranged as a sitting-room-cum-studio. Here, scarcely an inch of wall was not hidden by books or paintings. A number of sleek, portly cats blinked and yawned as the visitors entered.

'How did you know who I was?' Caspar asked, as the old lady closed the door and followed them into the room.

'You look like my father,' she answered. 'So did Alex, my eldest nephew. Rapscallions, both of them—not that Alex can be blamed for sowing his wild oats so prodigally. He was killed in his twenty-first year; and here am I, eighty-three, and not likely to die yet, it seems. Sit down. This room was not made for men of your height. Why are you here?'

While Caspar explained, Francesca's gaze strayed to a canvas set up on an easel not far from where, in response to their hostess's gesture, she had sat down.

It seemed they had interrupted Lady Alice at work on a still life. The objects which she had been painting were grouped on the table beyond the easel.

'I should have to bring the three cats,' was his great-aunt's reaction, when Caspar had put his request to her.

'By all means. Why not?' he agreed.

'Very well. I'll come over tomorrow, but only on trial, you understand. If I find Lanyon doesn't suit me, you will have to find someone else to gag all the gossiping tongues. Or marry the girl.'

Francesca felt a slow blush creeping up from her throat.

Caspar said dryly, 'She hasn't tried her wings yet. It would be a pity to cage her before she's had any freedom.'

'In my youth there was no such thing,' retorted the old lady tartly. 'A woman was always dependent either on her father or her husband. If I hadn't been able to paint, I shouldn't be free to this day.'

'What time would you like me to come for you?' Caspar asked.

'That won't be necessary, thank you. I am still in possession of a driving licence. You may expect me for luncheon. I won't offer you tea. I have a great deal to do between now and tomorrow,' she said briskly.

'Perhaps we could help,' he suggested.

'No, no—you would be more hindrance than help.' As she stood up, she looked him over and added, 'I'm glad to see you don't take after my brother or your father—not in appearance, at any rate. My brother was a selfish tyrant, and your father was the reverse, a spineless weakling. I never met your mother, but from what I've heard she was not a strong character either. However, you may have more backbone. You will certainly need it to succeed in creating order out of the chaos wrought by Osbert.'

'There's no doubting that old bird's backbone,' was Caspar's irreverent comment, as they drove away. 'I only hope she doesn't turn out to have a touch of tyrant in her make-up,' he added, on a slightly grim note.

Glancing sideways at his strong jawline, Francesca had no doubt who would be the victor in any clash of wills between him and Lady Alice.

'I wonder why she was in disgrace with your grandfather, and her name never mentioned?' she said.

'Ask Mrs Bray. I expect she knows.'

For the next few miles there was silence as they drove back by minor roads, stopping half way at a tea-shop in a quiet village with a river running through it and a family of ducks cruising upstream.

'Is all England like this?' asked Francesca, looking out of the tea-shop window at the harmonious combination of the architectural styles of many centuries.

'Not all. This part of the country is one that hasn't been spoilt by the horrors of high-rise building, or the depredations of modern farming. Not all the bees in my grandfather's bonnet were disastrous,' Caspar added reflectively. 'I'm inclined to think he was right not to allow any hedges to be grubbed out. There's strong ecological evidence that modern farming methods may eventually defeat their object.'

When they resumed their journey, he lapsed into silence again, and Francesca continued to ponder his answer to his great-aunt's embarrassing remark—*Or marry the girl.*

Caspar's reply had not sounded as if he had thought the suggestion outrageous. For one glorious instant of wishful thinking, she had wondered if he had come to be fond of her, too, and but for the gap in their ages might not be averse to the recourse suggested by the old lady.

But the idea was only a pipe-dream, and one better not dwelt on, she thought, with an unconscious sigh.

Caspar, who she had thought to be absorbed in the many problems besetting him, surprised her by taking one lean brown hand off the wheel and giving her leg a friendly pat.

'That was a deep sigh, *chiquilla*. What's on your mind?'

'I-I was thinking how lovely it is here ... and how safe,' she answered evasively.

'Safe?'

'No snakes. No poisonous insects. No piranhas or anacondas.'

'True, but there are other hazards.'

She didn't know what he had in mind, but she was suddenly reminded of Alethea Spencer saying, with a hint of coquetry, *Nothing to worry about on that score*.

I wish he would look at me as he looked at her, she thought wistfully, studying his strongly marked profile.

Caspar took his eyes off the road to give her a quick, smiling glance.

'I detect a certain unrest. A touch of spring fever, perhaps. At your age this time of the year does have that effect.'

'But not at your age?'

He heard the slight tinge of sarcasm, and it made him laugh. 'Yes, sometimes at my age as well. But this year I have other preoccupations.'

In spite of his suggestion, Francesca did not relieve her curiosity by asking Mrs Bray if she knew the reason why the old lady had been ostracised by her brother. She felt that, as an outsider, she had no right to pry into family secrets.

Lady Alice arrived at Lanyon at noon the next day. The lodge house at the West Gate was occupied by a gardener whose wife had been asked to ring up after opening the gate. Thus Caspar and Francesca were waiting to welcome her chaperone when she drove up to the house.

To their somewhat incredulous amusement, she was at the wheel of a Bentley, her three cats ensconced on cushions on the back seat.

'Oh, they wouldn't like that,' she replied, when Caspar expressed surprise at their not being in baskets. 'They've been motoring since they were kittens, haven't you, my dears?'—as she opened the door to let them out.

In a stately manner the cats descended to the gravel, arching their backs and stretching their front and back legs.

'I was thinking on the way over that you might care to exchange motors, Lanyon,' their mistress continued. 'Mine is very heavy on petrol and, although I don't like to be cramped, I think perhaps your little runabout might be more suitable for me, and this more suitable for you.'

'My little runabout doesn't belong to me,' he explained as, followed by the cats, and with Piper unloading her belongings, Lady Alice entered the house she had left more than sixty years earlier.

It was after lunch, while they were having coffee on the South Terrace, that she said, 'It might be wise to allow the impression to be formed that Francesca is under my aegis rather than yours. It calls for less explanation, don't you agree?'

'Yes, that thought had occurred to me.'

'You say you have met no one yet?'

'Only the Spencers' daughter, and she isn't to know that you haven't been here from the outset.'

'The Spencers? Oh, yes . . . of Mallington.'

'Not any more,' said Caspar. 'The Hall is owned now, so we hear, by a multi-millionaire called Carter.'

Francesca would have expected his great-aunt to deplore this turn of events, but instead she said, 'I shall be interested to meet him. Anyone who can make a fortune in these times must be a man of singular abilities. Do you wish me to call on him, or do you prefer not to mix with your neighbours at present? They'll probably call if we don't. I'm sure they must all be exceedingly curious to meet you.'

Her surmise was proved correct sooner than any of them expected. At half past four, when they were again on the terrace, having afternoon tea, Piper came to tell Caspar that the gardener's wife had given warning that Mr Carter and his daughter were coming to call.

'Are you at home, m'lord?' he enquired.

Caspar raised his eyebrows at the two women. 'Are we at home?'

Francesca said nothing. Lady Alice made a gesture which left the decision to him.

'Yes, we are at home, Piper,' he said.

When Francesca first met Daphne Carter, she felt an instinctive sympathy for someone so lacking in confidence, and so clearly incapable of making the best of herself.

Cyril Carter had plenty of confidence. He breezed cheerfully forward to shake hands; a small, stocky man from the Midlands, at home in any surroundings, neither self-important nor servile.

His daughter was different. Although she was in her late twenties, she seemed to be painfully shy. She had several good points, among them a lovely complexion and small, delicately formed hands with filbert nails. But her clothes and shoes were those of a dowdy middle-aged woman dressed up for a special occasion, whereas Lady Alice and Francesca were both casually dressed in cool cotton shirts with trousers.

In her synthetic blouse and spring suit, Daffy—as her father referred to her—found sitting in the sun uncomfortably hot.

'Shall I move your chair into the shade, Miss Carter? You aren't used to the sun as we are,' said Caspar, as her forehead and nose began to shine.

Being the focus of his attention made a wave of embarrassed colour suffuse her already pink face.

'It is rather hot today, isn't it? I wish I could tan like you, Miss Hartley. However careful I am, I always burn if I sunbathe. It's having carroty hair. You never see people with my colouring with a nice tan,' she blurted, in a nervous rush.

Caspar moved her chair into the shade of an old and
discoloured garden umbrella which, with the old-fashioned sideways-folding canvas chairs on which they
were sitting, Piper had disinterred from one of the store-
rooms.

'There, that should be better for you.' He moved his
own chair as well, not into the shade but so that it was
equidistant between her new place and Francesca's.

'I shouldn't call your hair carroty, Miss Carter. It's the
colour of satinwood,' said Francesca.

And indeed it was the same colour as several pieces of
elegant Regency furniture which she had admired during
a tour of the sadly neglected state apartments with Lady
Alice.

'Oh, do you think so?' Daphne looked startled and
pleased.

Then she gave a cry and, but for Caspar's lightning
reaction, her chair might have toppled backward as her
plump body lurched when the canvas beneath her gave
way.

'Oh . . . I'm *terribly* sorry, your lordship.' Her face was
now puce with confusion.

'It wasn't your fault. It's the age and decay of these
chairs,' he said, still holding the wrist by which he had
seized her and pulled her on to her feet. 'Have I hurt
you?'—releasing his grip. 'Still, better a bruise than the
crack on the head you might have had, had the chair
gone over.'

'Oh, yes . . . thank you . . . how quick you were,' she
said, gazing admiringly up at him.

The morning before Francesca had been struck by the
physical similarity between him and Alethea. Between
Caspar and Daphne it was their dissimilarity which
struck the eye; he tall and assured, she short, overweight,
as gauche as a girl half her age.

'Have my chair. This seat seems sound,' he said, bend-
ing to test the green canvas stretched across the seat.

In that instant, before he straightened, Francesca saw
in Daphne's eyes a sudden soft look which her intuition
told her was the onset of love at first meeting. It was clear
to her that, at long last, the millionaire's homely daughter was confronted with her *beau idéal*. And who was to
say that Daphne's yearnings were any more hopeless than
her own?

Dumpy and diffident she might be, but she was an
heiress and, as Caspar himself had said, many a rich
man's plain daughter had acquired a title and a mansion
by virtue of parental wealth.

Before the Carters departed Francesca heard Caspar
tell Daphne his first name, and invite her to use it. Possibly
this was his method of preventing her from repeating the
solecism of calling him 'your lordship'. Francesca's quick
ear for nuance had already made it clear to her that
Daphne should have addressed him as Alethea had the
day before. The respectful 'm'lord' and 'your lordship'
were for his staff, not his equals.

Yet when, upon taking his leave, Mr Carter invited
them to dine at Mallington, and was profuse with 'your
lordships', Caspar did not include him in the informality
he had established with his daughter.

'As I thought, a most interesting man,' pronounced
Lady Alice, when the visitors had left. 'The daughter
needs to lose weight, and she should do something about
her eyelashes. They remind one of pigs' straight, pale eyelashes. Otherwise not a bad sort of girl.'

Shortly afterwards Caspar returned from seeing them
to their Rolls-Royce.

He said, 'Apropos your suggestion that we should give
the impression that Francesca is under your aegis, Aunt
Alice, there is one flaw in the plan which didn't occur to
me earlier.'

'Indeed? What is that?' she enquired.

Before explaining, he said, 'Did it also strike you,
Francesca? When Daphne admired your tan?'

'You mean: Why are we both brown if I've been living with Lady Alice who's not brown?'

'Exactly.'

'No, it didn't strike me then,' she admitted. 'But I agree it's something which someone is bound to notice and wonder about.'

'But it can be easily explained,' put in his great-aunt. 'You have both been living in a hot climate—but not together. For all anyone knows your father's death may have been a recent occurrence. He consigned you to Caspar's charge and he, in turn, brought you back and put you in my charge. There's nothing unexceptionable about *that*; it's the length of time you've been together which might injure your reputation in some eyes, my child. Not in those of your own generation. The girl of today seems free to do as she pleases, fortunate creature.'

'In her twenties—yes. But Francesca is still very young. I should prefer that her reputation remains unblemished in everyone's eyes,' said Caspar authoritatively.

His attention was caught by something in the distance. 'I see we're about to have another visitor.'

The two women followed his glance, and Francesca recognised Alethea cantering across the park.

It was grazed by a flock of sheep belonging to one of the tenant farmers. They were kept from invading the gardens by a ha-ha, a deep, walled ditch, invisible from the house but forming an effective barrier. At one place it was bridged and gated, and here Alethea left her mount and walked the rest of the way.

The afternoon temperature being much higher than when they had first encountered her, today she was wearing a shirt of sky-blue cotton with a pink kerchief tied round her throat.

'Good afternoon. I've come to deliver an invitation from my parents,' she began, as she mounted the steps

leading up to the terrace. 'They——' She caught sight of
Lady Alice and stopped short.

As Caspar introduced her to his great-aunt, Francesca
found herself contrasting Alethea's assurance with
Daphne's awkwardness. She wondered what Lady Alice
would have to say about her.

But when, about half an hour later, Caspar returned
from walking with Alethea as far as the gate, neither he
nor the old lady made any remark about her.

A few days later the three of them dined at the Dower
House on the fringe of the estate owned now by the Carters. The occasion was a considerable ordeal for Francesca because, although she was not afflicted by shyness
in the ordinary way, at Sir Giles and Lady Spencer's
dinner party she found herself among sixteen people all—
except for their daughter—many years older than herself,
and all lifelong members of the somewhat insular coterie
of county gentry with whom, at first, she seemed to have
no point of contact.

From the asparagus, which fortunately presented no
problem because they had had it for lunch the previous
day, to the lemon soufflé, she struggled to make conversation with the two elderly men seated on either side of her.
But later, in the drawing-room, while sipping coffee from
a fragile porcelain demi-tasse and thinking wistfully of
the mugs of coffee she and Caspar had drunk after supper
on board *Rain*, she was approached by a woman who
said, 'I noticed you pausing to study the sampler in the
hall. Do you share my interest in old needlework? Lanyon
must be full of beautiful examples.'

From then on the evening was less of a strain because
she discovered that although, earlier, all the women had
seemed to ride or breed dogs, in fact there were one or
two present whose interests were gardening and needlework, and with them she could chat far more easily.

Afterwards, on the way home, with Caspar at the
wheel of his aunt's Bentley and the two women behind,

she was surprised and heartened to find that Lady Alice, although at ease in any milieu, had not found the evening wholly enjoyable.

'Politics—than which, as far as I am concerned, there is no duller subject—and reminiscences of wartime. Excellent food, but extremely dull conversation,' was her tart comment. 'What did you think, Caspar?'

'Mm, rather heavy going at times—particularly the woman with the weatherbeaten face and the booming voice,' he agreed.

But he had not found Alethea heavy going, Francesca had noticed. She had not been near him during dinner because he had sat on her mother's right, and she near the centre of the table.

But afterwards they had had quite a long tête-à-tête in a corner of the drawing-room, and she had made him laugh, not once but several times.

From the first time she entered the Long Library, it became Francesca's favourite part of the great house. More than one hundred feet in length, and said to house twenty thousand volumes in addition to a great collection of Old Master drawings, prints and manuscripts, it had tall windows all along one side and bookshelves along the other. A gallery gave easy access to the shelves near the painted ceiling. Being carpeted and furnished with many desks, writing tables, chairs, sofas and special stands to support large portfolios, it had a comfortable air in spite of its size.

But for Francesca its charm lay in the lustre of the gold tooling on the spines of row after row of fine morocco bindings, and in the smell of leather which permeated the Library and the two domed ante-rooms at either end of it.

One afternoon, she was curled on the floor of the gallery, deep in a book, when Caspar and his great-aunt walked in by the tall mahogany double doors at the far end.

As was nearly always the case, they were discussing Lanyon and its future. Francesca saw no reason to make her presence known to them. They were not having a private conversation and, if they left the Library by the doors at her end, they would see her for themselves.

However, as it turned out they came only half way along, and paused there for a short time—perhaps while Caspar looked for a book he had seen thereabouts—before returning to the far door.

And it was then, while they were out of sight beneath the middle section of the gallery but within her earshot, that she heard his aunt say, 'What you need, my dear boy, if you're going to run this place as it should be run, is a wife to take charge of putting the inside in order while you attend to the fabric, and the estate.'

'Yes, you're right. I've thought the same thing,' was Caspar's reply. 'Lanyon needs a mistress, and I need a wife.'

'And have not far to seek, I should have thought,' said Lady Alice.

'But not in the direction of Mallington.'

'No, no—I was not suggesting that. Although in a less extreme form, that would be to repeat your father's folly. I was not thinking of the Carter girl. The fortune she will have one day would be useful but less important, in my view, than a wife with charm and intelligence.'

'In my view, too.' From his tone, Francesca could guess at the gleam of sardonic humour which accompanied this reply.

'Well, on that score, Lanyon, you would surely agree that there is only one possible choice?—Unless you mean to seek your wife much farther afield than has been my impression.'

'No, but I'm not sure I should have expected you to agree with my choice.'

'Wholeheartedly! In your place I should act on it immediately.'

'I think not. I mean to hold my horses for some time
yet . . .'

They moved out of hearing, leaving Francesca's pleasure in her book and her surroundings irrecoverably shattered by what she had overheard.

So Alethea Spencer was to be the next Marchioness of
Lanyon, although not yet. Presumably Caspar's decision
to delay making his choice known to her was because,
although he accepted it as his duty to marry, he was in no
hurry to relinquish his personal freedom. That at least
was some comfort—or was it? How, even for Lanyon's
sake, could he bear to marry without love?

Charm was not a quality which Francesca would have
ascribed to his future bride. Intelligence, yes; and looks,
and the right background. But charm, no. In twenty-five
years' time she would be a replica of her mother, a
woman in whom could be seen a severity of temperament
as yet undeveloped in Alethea, but probably there none-
theless.

The next day, soon after breakfast, Caspar came looking for Francesca and, when he found her in the stable
yard, said, 'Harriet would like to talk to you. Rather
than keep her waiting while I found you, I said you
would ring her back.'

'I wonder why she wants to talk to *me*?' she said in
surprise.

'I don't know. She didn't say.' Caspar sounded preoccupied, as indeed of late he often did.

As she went to telephone Harriet, she could not help
sighing for their carefree life in the West Indies before the
burden of Lanyon had fallen on his shoulders.

'I wondered if you could possibly come to my res-
cue,' was Harriet's not very enlightening opening
remark, when they had exchanged the usual prelimin-
aries.

'Of course—but in what way?'

'Victoire, our au pair, has had to go home to hold the

fort there while her mother is in hospital. I wondered if
you would be willing to stand in for her—just for a few
days until I find a permanent replacement? The thing is
that we're on the brink of rather a whirl of entertaining
overseas clients, and I can't nanny them and the children. I know it's rather cheek to ask this of you, Francesca, but I'm really at my wits' end.'

'It's not cheek at all. I'd be glad to help. When would
you like me to come? Straight away, I imagine?'

'Is that possible?'

'I don't see why not. I'd better have a word with
Caspar and Lady Alice, but I'm sure they'll have no
objection.'

'I'm afraid I can't even offer to come and fetch you,'
Harriet said apologetically. 'But I've looked up the public
transport, and there's a choice of Green Line buses if
Caspar could run you to one or other of their stops.'

Presently, having jotted down the bus times, Francesca
went in search of him.

Finding anyone at Lanyon could take some time. As
she went about the house, looking in the most likely
places, she wondered how long she would be away.
Would he miss her at all, or would her absence be a relief
to him? Did he long to have her off his hands? If he did,
he concealed it. But she could not but be conscious that
she was yet another encumbrance on a man who, until
very recently, had been by temperament and choice a
lone wolf.

She was told where to find him by Piper, who directed
her to the attics of the west wing. There, in a warren of
musty, cobwebby rooms, she found Caspar poking about
among stacks of stored, dust-covered furniture.

'There are a lot of good pieces up here,' he said, when
she joined him. 'Better than much of the stuff in the
rooms we're using downstairs.'

Francesca told him the reason why Harriet had telephoned.

'No need to catch a bus. I'll run you in after lunch,' he said.

'Oh, no, please don't go to that trouble. I shan't get lost at the other end. Harriet told me to take a taxi from where the bus stops to her house.'

'It will be no trouble. I've several things to do in London myself. Give me a hand to move this table, will you? I want to get at a chair I can see at the back of this lot.'

For the rest of the morning she helped him to extract from the confusion of discarded furnishings a number of tables and chairs, and several fine clocks.

'Here you are: this can go in your room instead of rotting up here.' He lifted down a small table from the top of a chest of drawers.

The table top proved to be a lid with a misty mirror on its underside, and many small compartments in its interior. From two of these, at the corners, hinged flaps turned back to reveal gilt candle-holders.

'It's a French Empire work-table. You can keep your sewing paraphernalia in it,' he told her.

Francesca was enchanted. 'How do you know about all these things?' she asked, indicating the other pieces he had selected from the mass.

'For anyone at a loose end, particularly in winter, the museums in London are free, warm and quiet,' he answered. 'If one spends enough time in them, a good deal of knowledge rubs off. As a boy I spent a lot of time in them.'

Half an hour before lunch they returned to the lower floors, Caspar carrying her table and Francesca clasping one of the clocks, the rest to be fetched down later.

During lunch he told her to be ready by four, which gave her plenty of time to pack, and also lovingly to polish the French work-table. Years of neglect in the attic had dimmed but not destroyed its patina, and her pleasure in the table was intensified when she discovered that beneath the compartments was a drawer stuffed with all kinds of interesting bits and pieces from very small wooden reels labelled *Persian Thread* and *Glace Thread* to a pair of still-sharp embroidery scissors with handles of carved mother-of-pearl.

One evening, when she had been in London for nearly a fortnight, and was wondering how much longer it would be before Harriet engaged another au pair, Caspar rang up to say he would be there in ten minutes.

Francesca was alone in the house with the children, and had turned down the sound on the television before answering the telephone. Now she switched off the picture as well, and rushed to her room to make herself more presentable.

As in many London houses, the drawing-room was on the second floor, and she watched for Caspar's arrival from one of the two tall windows, conscious of quickened pulses and a sense of everything coming back into sharp focus after being slightly blurred for ten days.

He arrived by taxi and, as he stepped on to the pavement, and felt in the pocket of his trousers for change with which to pay the driver, she saw that he was wearing a dinner jacket. Clearly he was not dressed like that to spend the evening with her. He was going on somewhere.

As she went down to open the door her elation gave place to disappointment. To see him briefly was almost worse than not seeing him at all.

'Hello, Francesca. How are you?' he asked, as he crossed the threshold and waited for her to close the door.

'I'm very well, thank you. And you?'

'I'm fine, thanks.'

'You look wonderful,' she said, and then wished she hadn't.

It made his lips twitch with amusement before he bowed, and said, 'I'm glad it meets with your approval.

The shirt is mine, but the rest is on hire from Moss Bros. There hasn't been time to organise evening kit yet.'

'I'm surprised they were able to fit you—being so much taller than most people.'

'Oh, they can fit all shapes and sizes,' he said, following her up the stairs.

'And Lady Alice—is she well?'

'Yes. She sent her good wishes, and instructions for you to have your ears pierced.'

'Why should she want me to do that?' Francesca asked, turning a puzzled glance on him as she reached the second-floor landing.

'I think she has it in mind to present you with a pair of ear-rings on your next birthday. Judging by the number of women who have it done, it can't be too agonising,' he answered.

In the drawing-room, she asked, 'Will you have a drink? What would you like?'

'A gin and tonic, please. Shall I help myself? What about you? A glass of sherry?'

'Thank you.' She watched him open the lacquer cabinet which housed Sam's drinks.

Although she regretted telling him so, the white shirt and black dinner jacket were wonderfully becoming to his darkly bronzed face and hands. The hot weather they had enjoyed ever since their arrival had preserved their Caribbean tans, but Caspar's had always been the darker and, against half an inch of white shirt-cuff, his lean hands might have been those of an Indian but for their heavier bone structure.

Francesca was on the point of asking him where he was going, when he asked, 'Are you happy and comfortable here, *chiquilla*?'

'I'm very comfortable.'

'But not happy?'—this as he brought the glass of sherry to where she was standing on the mellow Persian hearth-rug.

'I'm not unhappy. But although there's quite a large garden here, I do sometimes miss the park and the woods.' And I miss you constantly, she added mentally.

'Yes, as long as this heatwave continues, I expect you will,' he agreed. 'But London has a lot to offer someone of your age. Aunt Alice and I have been talking things over, and we feel it might be a good plan if you were to stay on with Harriet and take advantage of some of the excellent evening classes that are available. You could take some day classes as well. Every girl needs to be able to stand on her own feet if necessary, and with shorthand and typing and perhaps a diploma in dressmaking, you would be qualified to do that. How does it strike you?'

It struck her like the knell of doom, but she hid her dismay, and said, 'Harriet may prefer to have a proper au pair.'

'I doubt it. If you put it to her tomorrow, I think she'll jump at the idea. In the ordinary way you would have a great deal more free time than you've had up to now while she's been particularly busy shepherding the Japanese people around.'

He gestured for her to sit down, then seated himself at the other end of the sofa. 'It doesn't always work out that way but, strictly speaking, an au pair is supposed to be treated as a daughter of the house, not as a full-time employee, and certainly not as an underpaid maid of all work. In normal circumstances, Harriet is a domesticated woman who only wants the children taken off her hands for a few hours each day.'

'Very well, I'll ask her,' she agreed. 'I know I must be independent. I've let you look after me for too long already. I—I had hoped there might be some way I could make myself useful at Lanyon.'

'Perhaps there may be—later on. Meanwhile it's in your own interests to acquire some qualifications, particularly as you haven't any of the usual bits of paper to prove you can read, write, etcetera.'

'Will Lady Alice stay at Lanyon if I don't?'

'Yes. She likes it, and I like having her. She seems to have none of the tiresome characteristics of her age; largely because she's in good health and her mind is occupied, I suppose. Anyway we get on well, and she's welcome to live at Lanyon as long as I'm there. How long that will be remains a moot point. I'm still taking advice on ways and means. The latest statistics produced by the Historic Houses Association aren't encouraging. Even Woburn is said to be losing between thirty and forty thousand a year. The only place which does seem to make a profit is Warwick Castle, which is owned by Madame Tussauds now. The crucial factor is tax relief——'

Caspar was interrupted by the telephone. As Francesca rose to answer it, he drained his glass, and said, 'I must be off. Call me at lunch-time tomorrow to let me know Harriet's reaction.'

'Oh, but this won't take a minute,' she exclaimed, with a gesture at the telephone. 'Must you go so soon?'

He glanced at his watch. 'Yes, I'd better. Can't rely on getting a cab at once at this time of night. Don't look so downcast. Your turn will come, Cinderella.'

With a pat on her shoulder, he said goodnight and departed to let himself out while, with a frown of vexation, Francesca turned to pick up the receiver.

By the time she had explained that the Scott-Leighs were out, and jotted down the caller's name and message, Caspar was out of sight of the windows. Francesca lifted his empty glass from the end-table and, on impulse, put it to her lips, although there was no way of knowing which part of the rim he had drunk from.

She guessed that most people would think it the act of a girl deep in first love, and so it was. But was first love necessarily ephemeral? Might it not, sometimes, last for ever?

She went to bed early, pondering the possibility that he

might not stay at Lanyon after all, in which case he wouldn't need to marry Alethea.

CHAPTER EIGHT

For the next few months Francesca worked hard at her studies—which included her mother's native tongue—made herself useful to Harriet, and learnt her way about London.

Once she overheard Harriet saying to a friend on the telephone, 'Oh, my dear, what a nuisance for you! All those problems are over for me as long as Francesca stays with us. The children adore her. She's utterly dependable, and we never feel now there's an alien presence in the house. I would keep her for ever, if I could. She's become like a younger sister. But of course she'll take wing eventually.'

It was lovely to feel wanted and valued. The overheard tribute warmed Francesca's heart, but it also made her conscious of how much more wonderful it would be if the place where she was needed was Lanyon.

Every other weekend she spent a night there; leaving London on Saturday morning and returning on Sunday night. But it was at Lady Alice's insistence, rather than Caspar's, that she made these regular visits.

Sometimes she would find a picture hanging in her bedroom which had not been there the previous time, or it might be a Regency footstool, or an ornament such as the opal glass cornucopia which she found on her dressing-table, filled with apricot roses from the late Lady Lanyon's garden of old shrub roses.

'Did you pick the roses for me, Mrs Bray?' Francesca asked, when she met her on the staircase.

'Yes, Miss Francesca. *Belle Amour* they're called—Beautiful Love. They were one of Her Ladyship's favourites. She once told me they were brought to England from a convent garden somewhere in Germany, but they may have been grown as far back as the time of the Romans.'

'And the vase—is that from her room?'

'No, I don't recall seeing it before. It's one which His Lordship found somewhere and thought you would like in your bedroom. Do you wish me to remove it tonight? Some people don't care to have flowers in the room while they're sleeping.'

'Really? I'd rather you left them. They have such a beautiful scent.'

That weekend she did not see Caspar until afternoon tea at four o'clock, a ritual no longer observed by the busy, weight-conscious wives of Harriet's generation, but one enjoyed by Lady Alice and also by her great-nephew. Usually, he had appeared on the scene before Piper had finished laying the table and lighting the flame under the copper kettle from which, when it boiled, Lady Alice would fill the Georgian silver tea-pot. But on this occasion he was late, and when he arrived he was not alone.

Daphne was with him; a very much slimmer Daphne than the last time Francesca had seen her, four or five weeks before.

'I went to a health farm,' she confided when, while Caspar was listening to something Lady Alice was saying, Francesca complimented her. 'I lost eight pounds in a fortnight, and another six pounds since I came back. But I've still got a long way to go before I'm as slim as you are—and I'm afraid I shall never be able to eat buttered scones and cakes again.'

'Oh, I expect you will, now and again, when you've reached your correct weight,' said Francesca. 'The family I live with in London are always trying out some new diet. Harriet's current oracle is Nathan Pritikin.'

'Who the devil is he?' enquired Caspar, overhearing this last remark.

'He's a nutrition expert who runs a Longevity Centre in California. He's written a book on his programme of diet and exercise which is a best-seller in America, and someone sent Harriet a copy. So now we're all on a régime of wholegrains and pulses, but no fat, sugar or eggs, and very little meat or fish.'

'I attribute my own longevity to eating *all* nature's good things, but only when they've been prepared in my own kitchen or by some other good cook. I eat nothing produced in a factory,' proclaimed the old lady.

'I should think you must have a very efficient metabolism, Lady Alice,' said Daphne.

The statement surprised Francesca. At one time all Daphne's contributions to the conversation had had to be prised out of her as answers to questions. She had never dared to volunteer an opinion on anything.

'I don't know about that. I certainly have a good deal more common sense than most people. I've never stuffed myself with pills. If I can't sleep, I read. If I were constipated, I should go for a brisk walk rather than swallowing a purgative. Try some of this excellent ginger cake, child'—this as she noticed that Francesca was no longer eating.

'Better not! It's full of forbidden ingredients. Harriet's oracle wouldn't approve,' said Caspar, with a grin. 'What about you, Daphne?'

'No, thank you.' She had turned rather pink at the old lady's reference to constipation.

She might have lost weight and gained confidence, but she had not shed her genteel attitudes, which must have been inculcated in her by her dead mother rather than her down-to-earth father.

Although, in a way, Francesca liked to be called 'child' by the old lady, because it gave her the feeling of being a member of the family, at the same time she felt it was a form of address which underlined her youth, and each time she came to Lanyon she strove to appear more grown-up and sophisticated.

Whether Caspar noticed any change in her was impossible to tell. His manner towards her never altered from one visit to the next.

It was not until she went down to dinner that night that she had a chance to mention the cornucopia to him.

He said, 'I'm still coming across trunks and tea-chests which haven't been opened for donkey's years. In the same crate as the vase for your room, we unearthed some bronzes for my room.'

'You and Lady Alice?'

'No, Alethea was helping me.'

How much time did she spend at Lanyon now? Francesca wondered. But although there were other people who could have supplied the answer to a question she would not ask him, she did not ask them.

That night, in bed, Francesca remembered Caspar's reference to 'your room'. She wished with all her heart that the bedroom really was her room. But although she might always be welcome at Lanyon as far as he was concerned, because he thought of her as a child and was unaware of her feelings for him, she knew that his wife was unlikely to be equally blind. Also once he was married, she herself would never willingly come to the house again. It would be intolerably painful to see him with a wife, even if the marriage was no love match.

For some time she had been trying to think of a tangible expression of her gratitude for his care of her. It was the scent of the *Belle Amour* roses which gave her the answer to the problem.

Mrs Bray was the only person to whom she confided her scheme. From her she learned of an old man, living in the village of Lanyon St Mary's, who had been a gardener in the time of Lady Lanyon.

As soon as she had a chance to visit him without anyone else knowing about it, Francesca went to see him.

Although almost blind, he still had an uncannily clear memory of all the plants he had tended. With his aid she was able to identify all the species growing in the rose garden from the one called *Small Maiden's Blush* to the famous French rose, *Viridiflora*, with blue buds opening into green flowers with brownish markings.

Having identified all the roses, she then spent some time researching their histories before writing a pamphlet about the rose garden. She gave this, faultlessly typed on an electric machine and bound in a cover she had designed and drawn, to Caspar for Christmas. By this time he had decided to open Lanyon to the public, and she was able to say, when presenting her offering, 'Perhaps a short extract from this might be worthy of inclusion in the Guide to Lanyon.'

He read half a page of the pamphlet before he looked up, and said, 'If you can produce something of this order, perhaps I shall commission you to write the Guide for me. You must have been hatching this for some time. We'll have it printed in full as an extra booklet for our horticulturist visitors.'

'Oh, no—it's not good enough for that. But I thought, knowing how fond you were of your grandmother, you would like to have her garden commemorated.'

'Thank you, Francesca.' He bent and kissed her lightly on the cheek, a salute which lit a glow inside her which lasted all the rest of the day.

But on Boxing Day they went to a lunch party at a house a few miles away where the guests included the Spencers. Watching Alethea and Caspar talking together, Francesca had a sinking feeling that now he had made up his mind to stay at Lanyon, his next move was sure to be the acquisition of a wife.

She did not see him at New Year because she had promised to help with the Scott-Leighs' party and Caspar, it turned out, had accepted another invitation before Harriet mentioned her party to him.

From then on she lived in the constant expectation of hearing that he was engaged. But as the winter months passed, and nothing happened, she began to hope that perhaps after all his sense of duty did not extend to the surrender of his freedom.

One night, after going to a party with the brother of a girl she had met at her Italian classes, Francesca did not get home till the small hours.

Swiftly she climbed out of the car, closing the door as quietly as possible in an effort not to disturb the Scott-Leighs and their sleeping neighbours.

To remind Robert not to take off with his usual exuberant boom, she bent to the window, her finger to her lips. He nodded. They exchanged final waves and, having waited to see her insert her latch-key, he moved off with a minimum of noise.

The red-shaded lamp on the table cast a cosy glow over the hall. Francesca closed the door, pressed the catch on the lock, and slipped the security chain into place.

'Where the devil have you been?' a low-pitched but irate voice demanded from behind her.

With a gasp, Francesca whirled round to see Caspar's tall figure outlined against the brighter light of the kitchen.

Where he was standing, the subdued lamplight did not reach him, screened as he was by the rise of the staircase. For a moment, until he moved forward, he was merely a male silhouette in the oblong of the doorway, but one which she would have recognised instantly, even if he had not spoken. Sam, although equally broad of shoulder, was not as tall, and had a shorter, thicker neck.

'Caspar! What are you doing here?' Her immediate reaction was pleased surprise.

'Waiting for you.'

As he advanced into the wider part of the hall between the front door and the curtail-step of the stairs, she was dismayed to see that his face was a hard mask of anger.

'I asked where you'd been.'

'We had a breakdown . . . two breakdowns.'

'Two?'

She licked her lips, suddenly nervous of this unfamiliarly grim aspect of a man she thought she had seen in all his moods, light and dark. But never had she seen him like this before.

'H-hadn't we better go into the kitchen? Our voices may disturb the others,' she suggested, in a nervous undertone.

Without replying, he stood aside for her to pass him. As she did so, she thought it was almost like passing a source of heat, so strongly did the force of his anger emanate from him.

Entering the kitchen, she said, with forced lightness, 'Oh, you've been making coffee. I must say I do long for a hot drink after all that hanging about.'

As she moved towards the cooker where a coffee pot was standing on an asbestos mat over a low heat, she heard the door being shut. But she was not aware of Caspar being close behind her when she turned aside to reach for one of the mugs hanging on hooks from the back of the dresser.

When her hand was arrested by his, clamping over her outstretched wrist, she gave another gasp—of nervousness now rather than the agreeable shock which had caused her first indrawn breath.

For the third time, he asked, 'Where have you been?'

'Caspar, please—you're hurting me!' she protested.

His grip did not slacken. 'I should like to turn you over my knee and give you a lesson you wouldn't forget in a hurry,' he said, through set teeth. 'Do you realise what time it is? Nearly three in the morning! You're supposed to be in not later than midnight.'

'I know I am, but——'

'But me no buts, girl. If whoever took you out tonight

has a car that's so bloody unreliable it breaks down twice in one evening, you've no business to be with him!'

It was the first time in their association that Francesca had known him to use even the mildest swear word in the presence of women. It was one of the things she admired in him—that he did not subscribe to any of the trendy cults, least of all the extraordinary vogue which had brought into fashion expressions from which, inwardly, she flinched.

She had no doubt that, with other men, his language was less circumscribed; but with her he had never said anything to offend a nun. His usual restraint made all the more forceful now his use of a word which, with some men, was a mere commonplace. His enragement baffled and frightened her. She could not understand it.

'If I'd known you were going to come here this evening, I shouldn't have gone out at all,' she protested, 'but anyone can have a breakdown.'

She made a futile attempt to free her wrist from the biting pressure of his grasp. Clearly he was too furious to realise that the steely strength of his fingers did not only hold her captive but caused her considerable pain. Pride forbade her to show how much. She wanted to whimper, but instead she lifted her chin and met his fierce eyes with a defiance she was far from feeling.

'Certainly they can,' he agreed, 'but anyone with a vestige of consideration rings up to explain a delay.'

'I did try to ring up . . . several times. But two of the kiosks had been vandalised, and when we found one that was working, the line was engaged.'

'Not during the past four hours. You could have got through any time after eleven.'

'Deliberately, I didn't try again after eleven. Sam and Harriet said they were going to have an early night because of being out so much earlier this week. I thought they wouldn't be grateful if I woke them up. How was I to know you would be here?—Sitting up for me like an over-anxious father,' she added unwisely.

The iron grip tightened and she winced.

'Where were you tonight?' he demanded. 'And with whom?'

'We went to a party at Hatfield. I was with Robert . . . Robert Bailey.'

'Who was giving the party?'

'A girl called Emma . . . a friend of his.'

'Were her parents present? Did you meet them?'

'No, I didn't. I think they were there, but in some other part of the house. It was quite a large one.'

'This man Bailey—how did you meet him?'

'Through a girl in my class. Really, Caspar, anyone would think you were a detective grilling a criminal! What on earth do you suspect me of doing?'

'I don't suspect *you* of anything. But I know you're a virgin—or were, before you left Lanyon. I'd hoped that Harriet and Sam would exercise sufficient supervision to ensure that you remained one. There are pitfalls here, for the innocent, every bit as unpleasant as those that drove you to masquerade as a boy in South America.'

'Perhaps there are, but I didn't fall into one tonight. Robert is a very nice boy. He didn't break down on purpose. It was——'

'You call him a boy. How old is he?'

'Two years older than I am.'

'He's no boy, he's a full-grown man. Don't you think it's rather ill-judged to go haring into the country with someone you don't know too well? Supposing the party had turned out to be a debauch? Such things have happened when parents turn a blind eye.'

'They may. They didn't tonight. It was an ordinary, harmless party. You're making a fuss about nothing.'

'I'm making a fuss because for nearly three hours— since you didn't arrive home at midnight as you were supposed to—I've been wondering where the hell you were, and what might be happening to you.'

'I've told you where I was. Nothing happened. Now I'm tired and I want to go to bed, not to stand here being bullied and badgered——' She broke off, almost in tears.

Every day she had missed him unbearably. Nothing in her life in London was compensation for not being at Lanyon with Caspar. Tonight he had come unexpectedly and, by the unluckiest chance, she had not been there to enjoy the rare treat of his presence. Now they were having a row. It was too much. She wanted to weep.

Instead, being predominantly English, she swallowed the lump in her throat, and hardened her voice, and said angrily, 'It's just as well I do live here. If I'd stayed with you I shouldn't have had any freedom. You seem to think I'm a child still. I'm not. I'm a woman now, and I can take care of myself.'

The flash of defensive anger died within seconds of flaring; but not before it had kindled a retaliatory gleam in the narrowed grey eyes above hers.

Before she knew what he was doing, he was no longer gripping her wrist but had her held fast in one arm while his free hand tilted her head back.

'If you're so self-possessed nowadays, show me how you would handle this situation, if I were one of your dates about to make an intensive pass at you.'

'N-none of them would behave in this w-way.'

Caspar gave a harsh laugh. 'An assertion that proves your inexperience! Any man will behave in this way. That one hasn't—till now!—has been luck.' He pressed her more closely against him, his hard eyes brilliant with mockery. 'You have precisely ten seconds to demonstrate how to avoid being kissed, my Francesca.'

Obviously enjoying her discomfiture, he began counting. Ten seconds had never seemed longer. She felt trapped; half afraid, half excited. Did he really mean to carry out the threat? Her own heart was beating fast, but if his was she couldn't feel it, in spite of being crushed to his chest.

The strangeness of his manner made her wonder, just for an instant, if he might have been drinking. But even as she thought it, she knew it was not so. He was as sober as she was. The devilish gleam in his eyes had nothing to do with whatever he might have drunk while awaiting her return.

'Please, Caspar . . .'

Her whispered plea might not have been uttered for all the effect it had on the remorseless countdown.

'. . .. three . . . two . .. . one . . . zero.'

As his head bent, she closed her eyes, her whole being braced to withstand a hard, brutal, punitive kiss.

But his mouth, when it touched hers, was gentle. It pressed warmly on her closed lips which trembled beneath it and softened in instant submission.

This was Caspar with whom, for months, she had lived protected and safe. How could anything he did alarm her? She had dreamed of his kisses . . . longed for them . . . imagined her fervent response. Here at last was her chance to prove her claim to be a woman.

His second kiss was not gentle. Her uncertain attempt to prove herself warm and eager seemed to unleash a fierce blaze of passion for which she was unprepared. With her heart already committed to Caspar, she had kept her relationships with other men on a friendly plane. Some kisses had been unavoidable, but although she had heard girls say that men quickly lost interest if they were kept at arm's length, her own experience had not confirmed this. She had even begun to suspect that the girls who said it were using it as an excuse for their own inclinations, and that some boys made passes on first dates because they felt it was expected of them.

At any rate the few kisses she had received, and the even fewer she had returned, had been an inadequate preparation for being kissed by Caspar.

Never before had she been held so close to a man, or by a man whose tall, powerful body made her realise the feebleness of her own strength. Nor had any of those who had kissed her been as old as he was, or half as experienced.

His mouth moved on hers with an irresistible persuasiveness which, had she not wished to yield, would have swiftly overcome her resistance. In that second long, sensuous kiss he taught her more about the joy of being a woman than even her eager imagination had been able to conjure.

She felt herself melting with pleasure, delighting in the steely compulsion of his arms, the unfamiliar small-hours roughness of his cheek against hers.

When the kiss stopped she did not immediately open her eyes, but stayed with her face raised to his, hoping that after a pause he would kiss her again.

Instead, he said, 'You see? There's no way a girl can defend herself against a determined man.'

But his tone was not angry any more. It was . . .

Francesca did open her eyes then to see if his expression had changed as much as his voice. As she did so, she murmured, 'But you're so much stronger than most men that it wasn't a fair demonstration.' And, seeing the change in his face, 'I don't think it was a demonstration. You *wanted* to kiss me.'

The effect of this statment was to make him release her so suddenly that she staggered back against the table while he swung on his heel and went to stand by the freezer, with his back to her.

Knowing she had rekindled his anger, and wanting to placate him, she said, 'I—I'm sorry, that was a stupid thing to say. I didn't mean it.'

The kitchen clock ticked for some time before at last he turned towards her.

'It was true,' he said with a frown. 'But we'll discuss that in the morning. Right now you should be in bed. While you were out Sam and Harriet had a call from Harriet's mother, whose husband has been taken ill. They'll be spending the night with her. They took

Lucinda with them, and I said I would stay with the twins until you returned, but I shan't drive home at this hour. I'll use the visitors' room.'

'The bed isn't made up. You'll need——' she began.

'I've already found the necessary bed-linen. Go to bed, please, Francesca.'

It was an order which brooked no argument. She said an uncertain, 'Goodnight', and did as he bade her. But it was a long time before she slept. Her mind was full of his admission that he had kissed her from inclination as much as to give her an object lesson.

In the morning she was wakened by Alice.

'Uncle Caspar is taking us to school today, but he said you'd better be woken up in case Mummy or Daddy ring up before he gets back. They might have an important message.'

The twins' schools were not far away, but they were on the other side of a dangerously busy road, so it was one of Francesca's duties to escort them there every morning.

When Caspar returned after deputising for her, she was downstairs, her hair brushed, her face lightly made up, and wearing the azalea-pink velours track suit that had been Harriet's Christmas present.

'Any word from Sam yet?' he asked, when she opened the front door.

She shook her head. 'Not yet. Thank you for organising the twins. Did you have some breakfast with them?'

Before he could answer, the telephone rang. It was Harriet. Her father was in an intensive care unit, and she was bringing her mother to stay with her until he was out of danger. She would be home for lunch.

Having relayed this news to Caspar, Francesca asked again, 'Did you have some breakfast with the children?'

'Yes, I did. Shouldn't you be on your way to a class?'

'No, this is one of my free mornings when I help Harriet.'

'I see. In that case I'll be on my way.'

'But last night you said you would . . . discuss things in the morning.'

'There's not a great deal to discuss, Francesca. However, if you insist, I'll stay for one more cup of coffee.' He gestured for her to precede him to the kitchen-cum-breakfast room.

She had rinsed out and refilled the percolator before he returned. It needed only a few minutes more for the coffee to be ready.

'You say "if you insist" as if you thought me unreasonable. But you can't kiss someone like that, and then go off as if nothing had happened,' she said awkwardly, when he had taken up a position, leaning against the cupboard with his arms folded, and seemed to be waiting for her to initiate the discussion.

'You've been kissed before, I imagine.'

'Not much . . . and never like that. If you wanted to kiss me, why are you hurrying away—instead of doing it again?' As she spoke, she went to him and placed her hands on his chest, her face raised to his, a shy, loving smile curving her lips.

Caspar put his hands over her smaller ones. Just for an instant she thought he was going to repeat the embrace of a few hours before.

Then, removing her hands from his body, he let them fall to her sides. 'Because I try not to repeat my mistakes, and kissing you was a mistake. I was tired. I'd been worried about you. You were looking more grown up than usual. So I lost control for a moment.'

'But Caspar, I *am* grown up now. I'm not the skinny thing I was when we met. Look at me—stock size twelve.' She smoothed the soft, loose velours to display the now rounded contours of her slender shape.

'Yes, you have a beautiful figure, but it would still be cradle-snatching on my part if I took what you're ready to give me,' he said dryly. 'You think you're in love, but it may be an infatuation. You've seen too little as yet to know where your future lies. People change and develop all their lives, but never as much as between eighteen and twenty-five. If I were still a free agent, perhaps I should have fewer scruples. But I'm not: I've taken on Lanyon, and that's a responsibility that precludes a lot of things I might have done once. I'm ready to settle down now, but you're not—not by some years.'

Francesca wanted to protest, *I am, I am!* But the words died before they were uttered. She knew his nature too well to think she could ever convince him that, because of her strange, lonely girlhood, her character was already firmly moulded.

'In that case perhaps it would be better if I didn't come to Lanyon any more,' she said, in a low voice.

'Don't be foolish. Where else would you go?' he said curtly. 'You will always be welcome at Lanyon. What happened last night doesn't alter that. It was only a kiss, for God's sake.'

Only a kiss. Only the most magical, world-changing experience of her life.

The percolator, left on a high flame, began to spurt jets of hot coffee from its spout. Caspar reacted more swiftly than she did. In two strides he reached the stove and snatched the pot off the heat.

'Is there a mopping up cloth?' he asked.

'Yes, but I'll see to it. Y-you pour out your coffee.'

A diversion had never been more welcome. Without it she would have had to go on standing there, mute with the mortification of finding that he knew how she felt about him, and that last night's ardent embrace had been of no more significance than his lovemaking with Beverley Vogt.

Caspar drank his coffee standing up. He must have put plenty of milk in it to enable him to swallow it quickly. By the time she had finished wiping the spattered hob and part of the adjoining work-top, his cup was already half empty.

He said, 'It's just as well we're ashore now. Had we still been living on the boat, the situation would have tried a saint—and I've never been a saint. Even now it's not easy to resist you, Francesca.'

She knew he was trying to salve her pride, but nothing he said could do that.

She stayed silent, and he went on, 'I'm twelve years older than you are. To involve you in any relationship but marriage would be rightly condemned by anyone with any morals, and marriage is equally out of the question. I've committed myself to a project that will be a considerable burden for at least the next ten years. You're too young to shoulder it with me, and in a year or two you'll be grateful that I wouldn't let you.'

'Shall I?' she murmured hollowly.

'Yes, you will,' he answered firmly. 'Now I must be off. I have a luncheon engagement on the other side of Lanyon, and various other things to do.' He came round the table and took her right hand between his. 'You know now that I find you very attractive, and I hope you know that I value your friendship. You're the one person who understands that I would rather not have inherited this responsibility. There was a time when your sense of responsibility for your father governed your actions, Francesca. Now Lanyon has to govern mine.'

When he had gone, she went slowly upstairs to strip the bed he had slept in and re-make it for Harriet's mother. He had left the bedclothes flung back and, on an impulse, she lay down and pressed her face into the pillow.

This was the closest she would ever come to sharing a pillow with him. Never again would he kiss her, of that she felt sure. And although he might have meant it when he said she would always be welcome at Lanyon, she had made her position there impossible.

Where else would you go?

She thought about it. Where else could she go? Was there really no escape from the misery of seeing him every other weekend, knowing he would never love her?

Suddenly the answer came to her. Not yet, not until Harriet's present worry about her father was over, but as soon as possible, she would go to Italy and try to find her mother's family.

She had saved nearly all the pin-money the Scott-Leighs insisted on giving her, and students could travel much more cheaply than other people.

As she rose from the bed, she felt no less unhappy and hopeless than when she had laid herself down, but at least now she had plans to make. It would not do to tell them beforehand that she was going; if she did, they might try to stop her. Instead, she would leave behind letters . . .

CHAPTER NINE

FRANCESCA met Jack Linslade at a party at his villa in Tuscany. He also owned a ski lodge in France, a house in Palm Beach and a penthouse in London. He was said to be a millionaire several times over—something to do with the silicon chip revolution.

Being told this about him reminded Francesca of Lady Alice's remark about Cyril Carter: that anyone who could make a fortune in these times must possess singular abilities. The memory of that hot afternoon on the terrace at Lanyon caught her unawares, as such thoughts still occasionally did.

She had been in Italy for a year by then, and while it had not been a happy year, it had been a full and interesting one. From the moment of landing on Italian soil, she had made a resolute effort to put the past out of her mind and to concentrate on the present.

Italy itself had helped her. Although to become a designer had been merely an ambition when she arrived, she had come to a country where design was important not merely to its practitioners but to the man in the street and, even more significantly, to the worker in the factory.

She discovered that, to the Italians, beauty was not some abstruse concept irrelevant to everyday life. They were, in a sense, a nation of art critics, and art they defined in its fullest sense to include the making of a shoe or a chair, or any other object fashioned by human skill, as well as the painting of a picture.

Her first concern had been to trace her mother's relations, and this had proved amazingly easy. Her mother's maiden name, supported by the device on the locket, had led her at once to a well-known family whose principal home was a villa a few miles from Florence.

In her careful, student Italian, she had written to her grandmother—her grandfather, she was told by a helpful librarian, had died a decade ago—explaining that she was alone in the world and, having no roots elsewhere, had returned to her mother's country of origin.

For a month there had been no reply. Francesca had come to the conclusion that her grandmother preferred not to re-open an unfortunate chapter of family history. She could understand this; had half expected it. Nevertheless it seemed oddly ungracious not even to acknowledge the letter with which, with the courtesy due to someone unknown to her, she had enclosed a stamped envelope addressed to the cheap *penzione* which was her first lodging in Rome.

One day she came back from work—she had managed to find a job as a waitress in a *pizza* restaurant—to see the unusual sight of an expensive car parked in the shabby *piazza* where she lodged. She might not have noticed the Alfa-Romeo except that her attention was drawn to it by the admiring comments of the crowd of small boys hanging round it. Had it been left unattended, they would not have been content only to look; there would have been grubby handprints all over the immaculate silver coachwork, she thought with a suppressed smile. She wondered for whom, in such a neighbourhood, the man at the wheel could be waiting.

'One moment, if you please, *signorina*.'

At first she did not realise it was she whom the driver was addressing.

It was only when he added, in English, 'You are Miss Francesca Hartley, are you not?' that she halted, and turned puzzled eyes on him.

He had climbed out by now, but was still standing close to the car; a man of about her own height, slightly built and classically handsome. He looked to be about Caspar's age.

'Yes, I'm Francesca Hartley. How did you know? Who are you?' she asked, walking slowly towards him.

'I recognised you. There is a painting in my house which might be a portrait of you, except that the hairstyle and the clothes are those of another generation. I am your cousin Giovanni, the eldest son of your mother's eldest brother. Since her father and mine are both dead, I am now the head of the family. You must forgive us for failing to acknowledge your letter, Cousin Francesca.'

His glance shifted from her face to their audience of children, and to a number of women leaning over the rails of the laundry-strung balconies of the surrounding tenements.

'We cannot talk here. May I take you somewhere more salubrious where we can make each other's acquaintance in peace and privacy?' he suggested.

Francesca hesitated. She had found out that Italian men were much more persistent in their attentions than Englishmen, and her short time in Rome had made her wary of the entire male sex because they were so quick to interpret a smile or any ordinary pleasantry as an invitation to fondle or pinch her.

However, there was no way in which this man could have known who she was unless he was, as he claimed to be, her cousin.

So she said, 'Very well,' and followed him round to the passenger's side where he opened the door for her.

'This is not a good neighbourhood,' he remarked, as the car moved forward and the children retreated.

'Perhaps not, but it's a friendly neighbourhood, and I'm able to practise my Italian more than I probably should be in a more select part of Rome,' was Francesca's reply.

There had been no double meaning in her answer, but he read one into it, and said, 'I can assure you that none of your relations intended to behave in an unfriendly manner towards you, Cousin Francesca. The reason I have not been to see you long before now is that I was away when your letter to my grandmother was delivered. It was some time before my wife discovered the existence of the letter. You see, my grandmother ... your grandmother also ... is now very old, and no longer in full possession of her faculties. Her eyesight was the first to go, which means that such few letters as she receives are read to her either by Gabriella, my wife, or by her maid who is almost as old but still active.'

He paused to concentrate on the heavy traffic for a few moments.

'Like many old people, my grandmother remembers her youth and middle years more clearly than the recent past,' he continued. 'She was unhappily married to a most difficult man, and at times she forgets that he is no longer alive to make life a misery for anyone who flouts his wishes. When her maid read your letter to her, she became very frightened in case her husband should find out. She ordered Maria to destroy the letter, after which she lapsed into a state in which she speaks only of her childhood.'

'Oh, dear—if I'd thought it would upset her to that extent, I should never have written,' Francesca exclaimed distressfully.

'I am glad you did,' was his reply. 'I am not a tyrannical despot like my grandfather, and I don't like to think of anyone of our blood being an outcast, particularly through no fault of their own. Fortunately old Maria's conscience was troubled by the secret my grandmother had imposed on her. Eventually my wife, who is very sensitive to other people's anxieties, persuaded her to reveal what it was that was worrying her.'

The road no longer demanding all his attention, he turned his head to give her a slightly smiling glance.

'I, being more benevolent than my grandfather but less soft-hearted than my wife, thought it wise to make your acquaintance before inviting you to join my household.'

'It's kind of you even to contemplate that, but it wasn't my object to sponge on you, Cousin Giovanni,' she returned, with a slight lift of her chin. 'I merely wanted to satisfy my not unnatural curiosity about my only relations—and perhaps to make friends to whom I could turn in any emergency. In the ordinary way, I'm quite capable of looking after myself.'

'But not, judging by your digs'—his English was far more fluent than her Italian—'in a manner appropriate to your position as my cousin. I applaud your spirit of independence, but I cannot believe you really enjoy your present work.'

There was a dryness in his tone which reminded her unbearably of someone else. In a city full of dark-haired men—although few of Caspar's height and build—painful reminders were frequent. The line of a prominent cheekbone, a glimpse of white teeth, a voice of a certain timbre even though it was not speaking English—every day some such detail would pierce her with an agony of longing for the man she expected never to see again.

'How do you know where I work?' she asked.

'I sent a boy up to find out if you were at home. Your landlady came down to speak to me. It wasn't difficult to find out a good deal about you. At first she was suspicious of my motives. You seem to have aroused her protective instincts. When I had convinced her that you had nothing to fear from me, she confided that you were a very nice, respectable girl. She thought it was not long since you had lost one or both parents. You gave an impression of sadness, she said. But according to your letter to my grandmother, your father died some time ago. Do you still grieve his loss very deeply?' her cousin asked.

'Signora Bari is mistaken. I'm not sad,' she answered untruthfully. 'The fact is that I wasn't greatly attached to my father. I'm afraid your grandfather was right in his judgment of him—although I still think it was cruel to cast off my mother because she made an unwise marriage. But I don't know both sides of the story—only my father's version of it.'

'You must talk to my younger uncle's wife. She was a close friend of your mother, and can tell you her side of the story.'

From that day on Francesca's existence altered completely. Giovanni and Gabriella took her under their extremely affluent wing, and would have liked her to lead the leisured life of a socialite which had been Gabriella's before marriage and motherhood.

When Francesca insisted that she must make a career for herself, and they saw she was not to be persuaded from that determination, they used their contacts and their influence to help her.

By the time she encountered Jack Linslade her Italian was perfect, she was infinitely better groomed and more elegant, and for the past six months she had been working as a general assistant in the house of one of Italy's most famous couturiers. It was a job which had been created especially for her because Gabriella was one of the designer's favourite and best customers, and it enabled Francesca to observe every aspect of the running of a great fashion house.

Before she met him she knew Jack Linslade to be a man in his forties, a widower with two teenage sons at a school in Switzerland. He was said to have loved his wife, and to be in no hurry to marry again.

'Nor, as far as anyone knows, does he have any other relationships with women,' said Gabriella, on the way to the party. 'He lives for his work now.'

Being somewhat similarly placed, Francesca felt predisposed to like him, and when during the evening he danced with her, and was neither predatory nor patronising but seemed genuinely interested in finding out what sort of person she was, she liked him the more.

His hair was prematurely grey, but still thick and curly. He had very bright blue eyes in a craggy, weather-beaten face. He was on the short side but well-knit. He radiated energy, and told her he needed only four hours' sleep. The rest of the night he worked or read.

When, two days after his party, she found him waiting for her when her working day ended, she was doubtful about having dinner with him.

'What are you afraid of?' he asked. 'That I may make a pass at you?'

'You haven't that reputation, but——'

'Maybe in twenty years' time I shall start chasing girls young enough to be my daughter, but it's not my present style. I regret not having a daughter because I like women's company. But most of the women I meet, unless they're happily married and therefore not free to dine with me, are mainly interested in my wealth. I don't think you give a hoot for that, I liked your curiosity about my work, and I'm interested in your plans. Does that reassure you?'

So began a friendship which both Giovanni and Gabriella thought could not possibly remain on that level for long.

It was largely because they would not give up trying to arrange a good marriage for her that Francesca accepted Jack's offer to finance a business for her. She believed him when he said there were no strings attached. She had not hesitated to accept because she had doubts on that score, but because it meant returning to England.

He wanted her there because it was where he spent most of his time, and what he would derive from the arrangement was her companionship when he felt like it. She was fairly certain that there was another woman in the background of his life who catered to his sexual needs but who couldn't listen intelligently when he wanted to talk.

The death of her aged grandmother was another decisive factor. With deep gratitude for their generosity to her, but feeling she had imposed on them long enough, Francesca took leave of her cousins.

She arrived in London with mixed feelings. Uppermost was her excitement at being able to set up a designer boutique with no money worries. Underlying this was her fear of coming into contact with Caspar. But London was a big city, and perhaps there was not too much danger that their paths would cross. She was more likely to run into Harriet.

On her twenty-first birthday, after a year of unremitting hard work, Jack gave a party for her. Ostensibly the hosts were a married couple who had been his friends for many years. Being a man in the public eye, he was anxious that no unsavoury innuendoes by gossip columnists should smear his innocent friendship with Francesca.

He often talked about Maggie, his late wife, to her. They had known each other from childhood. She had died in her thirties of an illness which the best doctors and the most advanced treatment had been unable to cure.

Once or twice Francesca had been tempted to confide her own secret unhappiness to him, but in the end she had kept her own counsel.

Everyone at the party was known to her, and all had a present for 'Franca' as they called her. Only Jack was privy to her real name. His present was modest: a book on the life and work of Mariano Fortuny, a designer he knew she admired.

A few days after the party she was reading *The Times*, as she did every morning at breakfast, when her eye was caught by the heading of an obituary notice. *Lady Alice Barrington*. She read it with tears in her eyes, for she had grown to love Caspar's somewhat eccentric great-aunt, and was sorry to have forgone her friendship during the last two years of her life.

She was leaving for Italy for a fortnight's holiday the next day, so she missed seeing the funeral notice in which the list of mourners would have been headed by the new Marquis.

Although it was necessary for her to subscribe to all the leading glossies, when looking through *Harpers & Queen* she was careful to skip the pages of *Jennifer's Diary* with its photographs and descriptions of upper class social events.

One day, when Francesca had been back in England for almost two years, her assistant Susie remarked that she and her current boy-friend had spent the day before, a fine autumn Sunday, at the stately home near his parents' house.

Off guard, Francesca said, 'Oh? Which one was that?'

When Susie told her, she stiffened. 'Did you enjoy it?'

'Yes, very much. You ought to go there some time, Miss da Rimini. It's a lovely old house. We took a picnic lunch with us, but we needn't have bothered because they were serving very nice meals in the Orangery.'

'Did you see anything of the owners?'

'There was a very tall, dark man who came out of a

door marked *Private* who Peter thought had a resemblance to some of the family portraits. But I don't think he can have been the Marquis. He smiled at us and said "Good afternoon". He was wearing a navy blue sweater and rather old jeans—I think he was one of the staff there.'

Caspar in the guernsey he had had since he was eighteen, and which was almost indestructible, Francesca thought with a pang.

Even now, after all this time, there was seldom a day when she did not think of him at all.

If ever she wanted to test whether she was cured of caring for him, she had only to spend an evening with another man. They none of them matched up to Caspar in any way. The only man whose company she did enjoy was Jack. She could relax with him, and they always had plenty to talk about. She had not yet repaid his investment to her in full, but was well on the way to doing so.

As her twenty-third year advanced, Francesca became increasingly conscious that, with the business established and her clothes lauded by all the most influential fashion writers, her life had lost direction and impetus.

What next? was the question which loomed over her, particularly in the lonely watches of the night when she couldn't sleep.

The logical answer was—marriage. But although she had only to telephone for two or three eligible young men to come running, the only man she felt she could bear as a husband was Jack. And he still missed his dead wife, and looked on herself as a daughter.

It was almost four years to the day since her heartbroken flight from England when she once again set off for Italy, and a holiday with her relations.

The day before Jack had flown to America on business. They had arranged to have lunch on the day after she came back, by which time she hoped to have shaken off her low spirits.

*

Normally, on the morning after her return from a holiday or business trip, Francesca would have been eager to get back to work. But this time she felt no such enthusiasm. Far from refreshing and inspiring her, the visit to Italy seemed to have increased her restlessness.

Instead of taking a taxi to the workroom, to see for herself that all was well, she merely rang up and talked to the dressmaker in charge.

Usually she brought back a spiral pad crowded with sketches and notes which she could hardly wait to incorporate into designs. But this time, although she had made notes, she felt no impatience to use them.

The career which had solaced her for so long seemed to have lost its power to absorb and content her.

The florist's assistant who came twice a week to arrange fresh flowers in the showroom brought white lilac for the window and jonquils for the writing table where customers made out their cheques.

When Francesca returned from the short walk to Harrods Food Halls where she had been replenishing her refrigerator, the scent of the jonquils conjured a vivid memory of the morning in the Home Wood at Lanyon when they had met Alethea Spencer.

They. Even now, after all this time, it was still fatally easy to think of herself and Caspar in conjunction; as if they had been a pair, instead of two people whose lifelines had run parallel for a short time, but had never merged into one as she had once dreamed they might.

'Aren't the jonquils pretty?' said Susie.

Francesca agreed, remembering another spring day, driving back from the visit to Lady Alice.

That was a deep sigh, chiquilla . . . *I detect a certain unrest. A touch of spring fever, perhaps. At your age this time of the year does have that effect.*

But not at your age?

Yes, sometimes at my age as well. But this year I have other preoccupations.

And I, four years older and wiser, should be concentrating on my other preoccupations, not wasting time being sentimental about a youthful infatuation, she upbraided herself, as she mounted the stairs to her tiny flat on the top floor.

Originally four pokey attics, it was now one all-purpose room and a minute bathroom. Always before, when she had returned to her eyrie after being away, it had given her a positive pleasure to open the door and re-enter the attractive setting of her private life, created out of the unpromising garrets.

But last night, arriving after dark, and touching the switch by the door which turned on three silk-shaded table lamps, she had seen her home from a different perspective.

Then, and again this morning, it seemed to her that the wall-to-wall ivory carpet and the pale fondant colours of the upholstery and cushions, chosen to make the room seem larger than it would had she used vivid shades, did indeed have that effect; but also they gave it a curiously unreal air, like a room-set in a magazine. Who but a woman alone, or an effeminate man, would surround themselves with these delicate tones of pink, blue, lemon and apricot and spread underfoot a carpet on which the smallest stain would be instantly noticeable?

Suddenly she had seen the room as a place where no child had ever scattered crumbs, no cat had ever kneaded the thick wool pile of the broadloom, and no ardent embraces had ever disturbed the arrangement of the cushions on the buttermilk Ultrasuede sofa which was also her bed.

A double bed, but one in which she had always slept alone, even if few people, judging her by her sophisticated exterior, would believe she had never had a lover.

Next day, meeting Jack for lunch at Ma Cuisine, she made a strong effort to seem more cheerful than she felt.

At least she had not lost her appetite, and the food there was of a standard which could, at certain times of year, make it necessary to book a table as far as six weeks ahead.

To begin she had *ofue Vert Galant*, a poached egg on sweetcorn in a pastry case covered with Béarnaise sauce, and Jack had the fish terrine. They exchanged details of their trips.

Suddenly, in the middle of the main course, for which she had chosen trout with tomatoes in a creamy saffron sauce, and he pork with prunes, he astonished her by saying, 'I should have enjoyed my trip a great deal more had you been with me. I've always been against marriages between people of different generations, but I believe we might make a go of it. How does the idea strike you?'

'It strikes me all of a heap, Jack,' she said, with attempted lightness. 'What a funny place to propose!'

For the tables, with their red checked cloths, were placed very close together, and their neighbours could, had they been listening, have heard what he had just said to her.

'I suppose it is. I'm sorry. Perhaps such a thing has never even crossed your mind. You're too young to settle for anything less than a big romance. I tend to forget how young you are. You look it, of course, but you seem much older in your ways than most girls of twenty-three.'

'As it happens it has crossed my mind, Jack. But I didn't think it had yours. But ... but now that you've raised the subject I know that, much as I like you, it wouldn't do. Not because of the difference in our ages, but because I still love someone else.'

'I knew that when we first met—but that's a long time ago.'

'You knew it?'

'Guessed it,' he amended. 'When you've been unhappy

yourself, you can recognise the signs in others. I could tell you'd been badly hurt. What went wrong? Or would you rather not talk about it?'

'Not to anyone else. I can tell you.' Keeping it short, she explained the reason she had fled to Italy.

'He was right, of course,' was his comment, when she came to the end of her brief account of her past life. 'A girl of nineteen and a chap of thirty or more are almost as many poles apart as you and I now. You've changed a lot since I've known you, and more since you last saw this man. Why not go and see him, Francesca? You might find that whatever you saw in him is no longer there.'

'I might,' she said doubtfully. 'But I don't think I ever saw life or people through rose-coloured glasses even when I was younger. My illusions were shattered in childhood.'

'You can't go on living in limbo, my dear.'

'No, I know,' she said with a sigh. 'I had come to that conclusion myself. I—I'm sorry I can't say yes to your suggestion.'

When they parted at the corner of Pont Street, she had a feeling that, although Jack had seemed to take her refusal in good part, it was bound to put paid to their friendship.

Not long after her return to the shop, Susie called her downstairs to the showroom to attend to one of their most important customers.

After Lady Cornwall had left, delighted with the shimmering dress which she would be the first to be seen in, Francesca stayed chatting to Susie for a short time.

'I must get back to work,' she said, at length.

As she went through the arch leading to the staircase, she heard someone open the door of the draught-lobby inside the street door.

She glanced over her shoulder, knowing that whoever had come in would be reflected in the huge Italian gilt-wood mirror on the opposite wall.

At the sight of the man who was entering, she froze, her eyes widening in disbelief.

It was Caspar.

CHAPTER TEN

FRANCESCA said coolly, 'How are you, Caspar? You look very well.'

He ignored this. 'I thought you were somewhere in Italy. How long have you been back in England?'

'I was in Italy for a year. The rest of the time I've been here. I——'

She stopped short as the door opened, and a fashionably dressed woman of about thirty came in.

'Sorry I'm late, darling. I got held up in Harvey Nichols. Hello'—this greeting to Susie.

'It turns out that your favourite designer and I used to know each other, Judith,' said Caspar. 'Her real name is Francesca Hartley. This is Judith O'Connor, Francesca.'

'How do you do, Miss Hartley.' The other woman held out her hand, her brown eyes bright with curiosity. 'When and where did you know each other?'

'A long time ago . . . in South America. How do you do?' replied Francesca. She turned to her assistant. 'If you'd like to take your break now, Susie, I will look after Mrs O'Connor.'

Francesca could not tell if Caspar's friend was wearing a wedding ring because her left hand was gloved, but it seemed probable that an attractive woman of her age would have had a husband at some time, if not at present.

Susie nodded and disappeared upstairs, leaving her employer to ask Judith O'Connor whether she was looking for a dress or separates, and if she had any colour preference.

'I wondered if you might have a top I could wear with a skirt that I bought here last autumn. It's a black skirt, of heavy silk, which is narrow down to the knees and then it has three deep flounces—rather like a Spanish dancer's skirt.'

'Oh, yes—I know which one you mean. Did you have the top that went with it? The one with the big, flouncy sleeves?'

Francesca watched the other woman unbutton her jacket, and would have helped her remove it had not Caspar forestalled her.

'Yes, and wore it repeatedly all winter,' said Mrs O'Connor, as she slipped the jacket off her shoulders and he held it while she freed her arms. 'But now I must rest it for a while. The trouble with your clothes, Miss Hartley, is that one tends to live in them. I've nothing I like as much as your black skirt and top, but one can't go on wearing the same things year in and year out.'

'I don't know why not. I do,' said Caspar, from behind her.

She smiled at him over her shoulder. 'It's different for men. You're not expected to ring the changes. We are.'

'Yes, indeed. If it were not so, people like me would go out of business,' Francesca said lightly. 'And although men always claim to have fewer clothes than women, and to make them last many times longer, the number of men's tailors and clothes shops doesn't altogether support that premise.'

It wasn't like her to chatter, and she strove for control of her nerves. Her hands were shaking as she flicked along the rail holding the separates, pushing the hangers aside and forcing herself to concentrate on which tops would team with the black skirt.

'These are two which you might like to try,' she said, turning back to her customer, and trying to ignore the disturbing third presence in the showroom.

The fitting-room was small, and it was her policy to leave people alone when trying on, unless they needed help with fastenings, or came out to ask Susie's opinion.

Now she wished very much that the shop had a roomier fitting-room so that she could closet herself with Mrs O'Connor instead of remaining outside while the other women tried on the tops which were Francesca's first selection for her.

Within seconds of his companion's disappearance, Caspar said abruptly, 'I introduced you as Francesca Hartley. But perhaps one of those rings is a wedding ring'—looking at the many rings adorning her elegant hands.

'No, all these are dress rings,' she answered. 'I am not married. But you are, I expect. Who was the lucky girl? Alethea or Daphne?'

'Alethea or Daphne? What the devil are you talking about?'

'I assumed you would marry one of them. But perhaps, later on, you found someone with beauty, breeding *and* money to be your Marchioness, Lord Lanyon.'

She could not keep the sting out of her voice. It might be unfair and unwise to slate him for choosing a wife with his head rather than his heart, but she found she couldn't help herself.

'Your assumption was wrong,' he said curtly. 'Both Alethea and Daphne are married, but not to me. I'm still a bachelor.'

'You are?' It was her turn to look blank.

'And likely to remain so,' he said grimly.

'Why do you say that?'

'I doubt if my reasons would be of much interest to you, Miss Hartley,' he answered, emphasising the formal address.

'I—I was sorry to read of Lady Alice's death,' said Francesca.

'Were you?'

The unmistakable scepticism of his tone made her say, rather hotly, 'Yes, I was—extremely sorry. I liked and admired her very much.'

'But not enough to write to her occasionally.'

'You must know why I never wrote. I couldn't trust you not to badger my whereabouts out of her, and then come and drag me back to live with Alethea or Daphne because, at nineteen, I was still so young . . . such a child still.'

'I knew where you were,' he informed her. 'Until you were twenty, I knew exactly where you were. After that——' He left the remark unfinished except for a shrug.

'How could you have known? I don't believe it.'

'First you lived in a *penzione* and worked in a *pizza* restaurant, and then your mother's family took you under their wing.'

Francesca's eyes widened incredulously. 'How could you possibly know that?'

'I guessed you would go off to Italy. Where else? But it cost me a great deal of money to have you tracked down and your movements followed. At the end of the year, I went over myself to check that you really were enjoying life as much as the reports indicated. You were! I spent part of an evening watching you dancing and flirting with a young man called Roberto Biagi in a night club called La Bussola.'

She remembered that night very clearly. The handsome, eligible young Italian who had fallen in love with her. Her attempt to be bright and vivacious, in spite of the ache in her heart—the unending, incurable ache.

'You were there. You were . . . near me. Oh, God!' she muttered, in a low tone.

'Having taken on a responsibility, I like to discharge it,' he said coldly. 'And it relieved Aunt Alice's mind to know that you were cared for and happy. She'd mistaken

your schoolgirl crush for a more lasting emotion. I recognised it as calf love, but I didn't want her to worry
that you might be eating your heart out. There was no
question of that. At the end of your first year in Italy, you
were having a wonderful time.'

Before she could refute this conclusion, Mrs O'Connor
came out of the fitting-room in one of the tops.

'I like this. What do you think, darling?'

It took Caspar a long time to answer, and Francesca
felt sure the woman was not so insensitive that she failed
to recognise that something other than polite small talk
had been taking place in her absence.

'It's very nice, Judith,' he said, at last.

'It does suit you, but perhaps you would like to try one
or two others before making up your mind, Mrs O'Connor,' said Francesca.

Her guesswork had been well founded. Judith was
wearing two rings. A platinum band on the third finger of
her left hand, which was clearly a wedding ring, and a
topaz ring on her right hand.

'No, I'm happy with this, thank you, Miss Hartley.'

Francesca said, 'The sleeves are a little too long for
you. To have it made up to fit you perfectly would take a
week or ten days.'

'That would be fine.'

Francesca measured the necessary alteration, and the
other woman returned to the fitting-room to change.

Caspar said, 'I have to take Judith home, but I'll be
back. Where do you live?'

'Here . . . over the shop. On the top floor.'

'I'll come back at nine.'

She lifted her eyebrows. 'Do your women friends like
these arbitrary manners, Lord Lanyon?'

She saw the muscles at his jaw clench. 'If you call me
that again, I——' He broke off and, after a visible effort
to control his annoyance, said coldly, 'Do you have an
engagement tonight which you can't put off?'

'No, as it happens I'm free this evening.'

'Then I trust you will have no objection if I call on you at nine o'clock. I shall try not to take up too much of your time, but there are some questions I should like to have answered,' he said, in a tone of arctic courtesy.

She hesitated. If she refused to see him, he couldn't force himself on her—or could he? At the moment he looked capable of murder. Why was he so fiercely angry?

'Very well,' she said, equally icily.

Then she turned away to make out a receipt for the emerald silk blouse appliquéd with turquoise and purple which Mrs O'Connor was buying.

When, about ten minutes later, Susie came downstairs, she found her employer sitting at the writing table with both hands covering her face.

'Miss da Rimini, are you all right?' she exclaimed.

Francesca lifted her head. 'Yes ... quite all right, thank you, Susie,' she said, rather dazedly. 'It was just ... such a shock to meet Lord Lanyon like that ... after so long.'

The girl said, 'When Peter and I went to see the house, and you asked me if we'd seen Lord and Lady Lanyon while we were there, you didn't tell me you knew him.'

'No ... well, knowing him was something I was trying to forget.' On an impulse at variance with her usual reserve, Francesca added, 'Years ago, when I was young, I was in love with him.' And still am, and always shall be, God help me, she thought.

'It can't have been so long ago. You're still young,' said Susie.

Francesca gave her a wan smile. 'Every year seems like five when you've found the one man who's right for you, but you're not the right one for him.'

'It doesn't seem that he picked the right one for him anyway. By the way she called him darling, I concluded that he and that lady were good friends, as they say.'

'Yes, it looked like it, I agree. But he isn't cheating a

wife. He hasn't one. I don't know why he's still single, but that's the way it is, apparently.'

'Perhaps he decided later that you *were* the right one, Miss da Rimini.'

Could it be that? Could it possibly be that? No, no—on false hopes like that a bruised heart could finally break.

Francesca shook her head. 'I'm afraid not, Susie. He knew how I felt about him and, although I wasn't aware of it until just now, after I'd gone away to get over him, he knew where to find me.'

The entrance of another customer put an end to their conversation, and Francesca went up to the studio. Knowing that she couldn't settle to anything, and feeling she was going to need every ounce of moral support to face Caspar at nine o'clock, she telephoned the salon where she had her hair done and asked to speak to her stylist. He agreed to fit her in between his last two clients of the day.

That arranged, she began to consider what to wear for the confrontation. The white suede trouser suit she had brought back from Italy? The poppy red crepon dress? A silk shirt and a plain black skirt?

Suddenly she thought of her newest design: the shimmering ocean-coloured evening dress. Why not? Why not look a knock-out, and show him just what he had missed? she thought with a rush of defensive pride.

She was ready by eight o'clock, with nothing to do but to pace nervously back and forth, wondering if it had been an act of folly to dress up like this. Although people told her she was a beauty, she never thought of herself as one; but tonight it would have been false modesty not to recognise that, aided by the dress and the skill of her stylist, and perhaps by the nervous tension building inside her, she did have a certain something.

At half past eight someone rang the bell of the street door, making her jump. She went to the entryphone.

'Who is it?'

'Caspar.'

'Please make sure you close the door properly.' She pressed the button that would unlock it for him.

The door of her flat was unlocked. She took a last look at her reflection, seeing green eyes bright with apprehensive excitement, ivory breasts exposed by the low décolletage which were suddenly rising and falling much more noticeably than they had been before the bell rang, and red lips which looked moist under their careful application of glossy lipstick but which all at once felt as dry as her constricted throat.

She heard him come up the second flight of stairs in three or four long-legged leaps, and rap an imperative tattoo on the door.

Feeling sick with nervousness, she inhaled a deep breath to calm herself, took up the position she had decided on, and called, 'Come in.'

As he strode into the room it gave her an insight into the feelings of an inexperienced matador when the bull was released into the ring or, perhaps more aptly, a Christian on seeing a large lion let loose.

Caspar saw her reflection in the large mirror opposite the door before he saw her. She was pretending to be putting the final touches to an arrangement of long-stemmed red rosebuds. She had bought them herself on leaving the hairdressers, but she hoped he would think they were from a man.

'You're early,' she said. 'Does Mrs O'Connor live in London or outside it?'

Caspar swung to face her, his grey eyes raking her from head to foot and back again.

Ignoring her question, he said with a sardonic gleam, 'Do you usually dress like that for an evening at home?'

'You said you wouldn't be here long. There's a party I may go to later.' Francesca stopped fiddling with the flowers and picked up a glass containing a colourless fluid and a sliver of lemon which probably he took for gin and tonic but which was in fact only spa water. 'Will you have something to drink?'

'A small whisky and soda if you have it?'

He took off his Burberry, which she recognised as one he had bought during her time at Lanyon, and tossed it over a chair. As she fixed his drink, she saw him looking around him.

'Thank you. Do you live here alone?' he asked, when she handed him the whisky.

'It's too small for more than one person. I told you this afternoon I wasn't married.'

'Many people aren't nowadays. It doesn't always mean they live alone.'

'It does in my case. I'm wedded to my career.'

'And have been phenomenally successful in a very short time, I understand, but'—again that bold, undressing look so unlike the Caspar she remembered—'it seems a waste of your other assets to give all your time to it. I can't believe that you do. Nor do I believe that you're dressed for a party. I wasn't born yesterday, my dear. You're got up like that for my benefit. Although, the way you've grown up, you don't need any artificial aids to make you desirable. You were lovely the last time I saw you at that club in Italy, but nothing to what you are now, and I'm quite sure you know it.'

After handing him his drink, Francesca had withdrawn to a chair on the far side of the room. Now, Caspar put down the whisky which he had not yet tasted, and came slowly towards her, his grey eyes narrowed and gleaming with what, with an uprush of panic, she recognised as desire.

As she sat there, momentarily immobilised by the clarity of his intentions, he took her glass from her hand and placed it on a nearby table. Then he reached for her wrists and, as he drew her to her feet, he said, with a sneer in his voice, 'However, since you've been to such pains with the wrapping, it would be churlish to refuse the present.'

She came to life then, but too late. As she would have wrenched her wrists free, he whipped them behind her. As she opened her mouth, he stopped her protest with a kiss.

It was the longest, most shattering kiss she had ever received and before it was over he was no longer holding her prisoner. Her arms were free—and round his neck.

Other men she could resist without difficulty. But there never had been, and never would be, any way she could resist this one man, not once she was in his arms with his warm mouth seducing her will.

Even when he said, in a voice now husky and slurred with passion, 'You'd better show me how this lovely thing you're wearing undoes. I don't want to do any damage,' her anger did not revive.

She was his. She had always been his. If he wanted to take her, here and now, how could it be wrong? Except that—

'No . . . please, Caspar . . . wait——' she began.

'I have waited—four endless years. Now I've found you again, and this time I'm not bound to refuse what you offered me once before. You're a full-grown, beautiful woman. I want you like hell, and I'm going to have you.'

He kissed her again, holding her with a strength which was at once painful and bliss beyond words. She felt him searching vainly for a zip at the back of her dress.

Reluctantly, she freed her mouth. 'Darling, let me undo it,' she whispered.

As his powerful embrace slackened slightly and she drew back to undo the fastener, which was in the side seam, she said unsteadily, 'The only thing is, it will be the first time for me, and it would be rather a disaster if . . . if I were to have a baby.'

Caspar was kissing the side of her neck as she spoke, and at first she thought he hadn't heard her, or was too swept by passion to care what the outcome might be.

Then she felt him tense, and he straightened and looked at her.

'A baby?' he echoed.

'It has been known, I believe. But perhaps you . . . that is . . . oh, dear!'

This last exclamation signified her distress at spoiling the exaltation she had felt a few moments ago. This was not how she'd dreamed it would be, in the days when she still dreamed about him.

'Are you telling me you're still a virgin?' Caspar asked on a note of incredulity.

'Yes.'

'I can't believe it,' he muttered. 'A girl as lovely as you are! God, you must have had dozens of men trying to take you to bed.'

'Not dozens. A few. I haven't been out with many men. I told you, I've been intent on my career.'

'But you're twenty-three now. Surely, even if you haven't known a lot of men, you must have met one or two who were acceptable as lovers? You certainly don't kiss like a girl who's deficient in sexuality.'

'I'm not—at least I don't think so. But I've never wanted just sex. I wanted love with it, and that was impossible.'

He was looking at her quite differently now. The hot fierce light of desire had gone out of his eyes. His gaze was intent and searching, shot through with puzzlement.

'Why impossible?' he asked

All her deepest emotions were very close to the surface.

'Because . . . because I'm a one-man woman, and I've never stopped loving you. Oh, damn you, Caspar . . . damn you for making me tell you!'

With a stifled sob she rushed past him to collapse in tears on the sofa. Heedless of her hair or her make-up, or the pale almond pink silk cushion in which she had buried her face, she wept with long shuddering sobs at the cruel trick of fate which had brought him back into her life.

She felt him sit down beside her and put his hand on her shaking back. She wished he would go away. He surely couldn't imagine she would let him sleep with her now, not after admitting that she loved him.

The moment of total surrender he had made her feel in his arms was over; a madness she would have regretted tomorrow, waking up to the knowledge that it was only her body he had wanted, not her heart.

It was a long time before her weeping ceased and she lay with her face still hidden, exhausted by the storm of misery.

Caspar was still there, sitting beside her, his hand on her shoulder.

'Listen to me, Francesca,' she heard him say quietly. 'It's no use my trying to pretend that I'm a one-woman man, because you know it isn't true. There were women before I knew you, and in the last four years I've had some casual relationships with others who, like myself, didn't want to become too involved. This afternoon you asked me why I expected to remain unmarried. The answer was because the only woman I had ever wanted to be my wife was very young when I knew her. Later she ran away, and after a year I lost track of her. For a long time I hoped she might come back, but eventually I was forced to conclude she never would.'

As he finished speaking his hand moved to grip her shoulder and make her turn over.

Although she knew she must look a wreck with smudged mascara and tear-wet cheeks, there was an unbelievably tender expression on his face as he went on, 'I didn't know I was in love with you until after you'd gone. I came here tonight thinking you'd become a sophisticated career woman and had probably had several lovers. To find you unchanged in every way, except in being even more beautiful, is so extraordinary that I can't take it in yet. Do you really still love me enough to marry me?'

Francesca lay among the heaped cushions and gazed at him with wondering eyes.

'Enough? Oh, Caspar, if only you knew how much I love you! To be married to you would be . . . heaven.' Her voice broke, fresh tears brimmed over.

He slipped both arms underneath and lifted her up to cradle her head to his shoulder. His mouth to her forehead, he murmured, 'Don't cry, my sweet girl, my lovely. It's all over now. We're together. Everything's fine.'

Presently, comforted, soothed, and happier than she had ever been in her life, Francesca lifted her lips to be kissed.

Some time later he put her away from him, saying, 'This won't do. It was difficult for me to resist you when you were nineteen. But now——' He stood up and crossed the room to look at one of her paintings.

She knew it was an exercise in self-discipline, and she loved and admired him all the more for being able to exercise that kind of command over himself; for knowing that this wasn't the right time to consummate a love so long and painfully deferred.

Later, while she washed her face and changed into a silk housecoat, Caspar foraged in her kitchen for the makings of a scratch supper.

'What I can't understand is why you had this crazy idea that I should be married to Alethea or Daphne,' he said, as they shared a large mushroom omelette with salad and wholemeal bread rolls.

Francesca told him about the day she had been in the Library and heard Lady Alice say he had not far to seek a wife.

'But, my dear girl, it was you she meant. She thought that in a few years you would be an outstanding beauty, with character and kindness as well. She didn't realise you were also extremely talented. What about your career, Francesca? Are you going to be able to run things from Lanyon? I must admit I don't fancy having a week-end wife only.'

'Blow my career,' she answered inelegantly. 'My staff won't suffer if I retire. There's a shortage of people with their skills. They'll be snapped up by other designers.' She paused, reluctant to strike a sour note. 'Judith O'Connor . . . is she one of——'

'No, she isn't,' he answered firmly.

'She called you "darling", so I wondered.'

'Judith calls everyone darling—her invalid husband, her teenage stepchildren, her friends. It's some time since there was anyone in my life but the ghost of a girl called Francesca,' said Caspar, reaching across the table to take her hand. 'Hence my somewhat intemperate behaviour earlier on.'

'You can stay here tonight if you like,' she said, rather shyly.

His lean fingers tightened on hers. 'No—not because I don't want to, but because, having waited four years, I can wait a little longer. I'll spend the night at my club, and tomorrow we'll meet for a leisurely Edwardian breakfast in the Park Room at the Hyde Park Hotel where I used to meet my grandmother as a schoolboy. Then we'll go to my bank and you can look through the family jewels to see if any of the rings appeal to you as an engagement ring. Or you might prefer to design one yourself.'

He paused to turn her hand over and press a kiss into the palm.

'After which we'll announce to the world that the marriage will shortly take place between the lucky Marquis of Lanyon and the lovely Miss Francesca Hartley.'

They were married by the Vicar of Lanyon St Mary's in the private chapel at Lanyon.

The wedding took place in the morning, some of the

guests, who included all Francesca's employees, having arrived the night before for a dinner party in the magnificence of the State Dining Room.

There had not been time for her to design herself a wedding dress. When her cousin Giovanni, who had flown from Italy to give her away, came to the room in which she had spent her last night as a single woman, he found her wearing a dress by one of her rivals.

It had not been made for a wedding, but for a summer evening party. Of white chiffon mounted on crêpe-dechine, it was a strapless sheath flaring into fullness from mid-thigh to just below knee-length. It could be worn on its own, or with a blouson of unlined chiffon with a crêpe-de-chine collar and cuffs. For her wedding she was wearing the blouson.

Earlier her London hairdresser had arranged her hair, as he had for the party. Last night she had worn some Chinese butterfly pins of iridescent enamel, but this morning their place was taken by white jonquils from the Home Wood. She had picked them herself, slipping out of the house as the sun was rising, before anyone else was about.

'I have been admiring the portraits of all the previous Marchionesses,' said her cousin, when he came to see if she was ready to go down. 'Some of them were good-looking women, but you are the first beauty in the family.'

Francesca laughed. 'I'm not really beautiful, Giovanni. Do you know the expression "it's all done by mirrors"? In my case it's all done by happiness. I've been on cloud ten ever since Caspar told me he loved me.'

'Gabriella says you mean to give up your career for him?' her cousin remarked.

He and his wife had arrived only shortly before the party, and there had been little opportunity for private conversation with either of them until Gabriella had come to her room for half an hour while Francesca was breakfasting there.

If she had obeyed Caspar's instructions, she would have had breakfast in bed; but having been out in the woods to gather the flowers for her hair, she had eaten her muesli and haddock at a table by the window.

'Yes, I couldn't be Franca da Rimini *and* Caspar's wife,' she replied. 'He needs my help here. There'll be plenty of scope for my talents, such as they are. I daresay it won't be too long before I'm designing children's clothes. I'm basically very domesticated. It was only unrequited love that drove me into the ranks of the career women.'

As she entered the chapel on his arm, she was conscious of many faces turned in her direction, and of the scent of white lilac being stronger than the smell of the cedarwood with which the chapel was panelled.

The scene of a number of funerals, and of innumerable morning prayers and services, when the family had sat in the two rows of upholstered chairs which faced each other across the aisle with the servants on hard chairs behind, it had never before been the setting for a wedding.

All the previous Lanyon brides, being themselves the daughters of peers, had been married in fashionable churches in the presence of large congregations.

But Caspar had said that he did not care what people thought, or who was offended by not being among their few guests: he had waited for her long enough.

With Sam at his side, as best man, he watched her come slowly towards him. Both men were in grey morning suits, but she was only dimly aware of Sam's presence and that somewhere nearby would be Harriet.

For Francesca, at that moment, they were all as insubstantial as ghosts. The only real person was Caspar, smiling into her eyes in a way which made her wonder how she could have endured the long years of separation.

She had remembered to transfer her emerald engagement ring to her right hand. As she withdrew it from

Giovanni's arm, and stepped forward while he passed behind her to take his place on her left, she could not resist an impulse to stretch out her hand to her bridegroom and feel his strong grasp for a moment.

Probably it wasn't correct, and would have shocked all her predecessors. His reaction was not only to take her hand in his, but to incline his dark head and then press a kiss on her fingers.

It was an act of homage that moved her deeply. The last trace of doubt that she was the right bride for him was dismissed by the courtly gesture.

But it was not homage but a fiercely possessive ardour that she saw in his eyes some hours later, when the celebrations were over and the last of their departing guests were disappearing in the direction of the West Gate.

She had waved them on their way with Caspar's arm loosely round her waist; but now, as he looked down, it tightened, and he pulled her close to his side.

'As soon as we come back from our honeymoon, I must have you painted, my lovely girl.'

'How long shall we be away?' she asked.

All she knew of his honeymoon plans was that they were to spend their wedding night at Lanyon, and travel the following day. He had promised her that she would like wherever he had chosen, and she had replied—and meant it—that a weekend in Wigan would suit her, as long as he was with her.

'A month at least—possibly longer.'

'Can you spare all that time?'

In the hectic week of their engagement, she had already discovered how many duties and how little leisure he had. A glance through the pages of his desk diary showed a working week of never less than sixty hours, the days filled with varied appointments such as 'tour new plantation', 'see farm manager', 'conference with accountants', 'discuss condition of tapestries with textiles conservationist.'

Soon the latter type of appointment would fall within her province, but even with the large staff he had built up, and her to share his responsibilities, the balance of his life would always incline towards duty rather than to the leisure and luxury of his forebears.

'I've given four years to this place, it won't fall apart in four weeks. Are you aching to know where I'm taking you?' he asked, with a smile, as they turned to go into the house.

'I'm curious. Who wouldn't be?'

'All right, I'll tell you. We're going back to Antigua, to cruise from there to Grenada.'

'Caspar! How lovely ... how perfect! Not on *Rain*? You don't still own her, do you?'

'Yes. I could never bring myself to sell her—just in case you ever did come back to me. Which reminds me, I've another surprise for you. It's up in our room.'

'Which is our room?' she asked, as he took her by the hand and began to run up the Great Staircase.

'For tonight we're sleeping in Kent's bed. When we come back you can have one of the rooms in the private wing redecorated to suit your taste.'

Francesca remembered Kent's bed. The finest of all Lanyon's State beds, it had cost many thousands, even in the eighteenth century. The bills for the velvet hangings, and the gold galloon trimmings, had been preserved in the archives.

But that last time she had seen the Blue Velvet Bed-chamber with its tapestried walls and bacchanalian painted ceiling, it had smelt neglected and musty, and the bed itself looked lumpy.

Leaping up the staircase left her too breathless to express any doubts about Caspar's choice, and before they came to the room he gave her a teasing look and said, 'It's no longer the original mattress, you'll be happy to hear. What was all right for princes and dukes won't do for American millionaires. We don't give them central heating at their usual level, because it would ruin the furniture, but we do give them modern mattresses and electric blankets.'

'You let them sleep in the State beds?'

'Why not, if it helps to preserve the beds for posterity?'

He opened the door of the Bedchamber, which now smelt of beeswax and fresh flowers.

Francesca went to the foot of the bed and stood looking up at the elaborate design on the underside of the canopy. The velvet curtains, once dulled by dust, had recovered their silken sheen. The gold fringes, though tarnished with age, had a refreshed look.

Caspar stood behind her and said, 'An architectural historian who came here to write the place up after I'd opened it described this as "possibly the most sublime bed ever designed". I don't know if anyone else has ever spent a sublime night in it, but I'm expecting to, tonight.'

Francesca turned, her eyes shining. 'And I, my dear love,' she whispered.

He caught her close, and his mouth roved over her face, savouring the smooth, soft texture of her skin, the delicate modelling of her eyelids. Her lashes fluttered under his lips. Her hands, which were trapped between them, could feel the fast thud of his heartbeats matched by her own.

It was dark when she woke up, still with her head on his shoulder. But the darkness was not impenetrable. Spring moonlight was flooding through the windows.

Caspar had woken before her. She could feel him playing with her hair from which, before he undressed her, he had taken the combs and the jonquils.

'What time is it, Caspar?' she murmured.

'About ten or eleven, I suppose.'

'Won't they think it strange . . . our disappearance?' By "they" she meant his personal staff.

'Not unless they've forgotten their own weddings. I

asked for some supper to be left for us in the Cabinet. You must be hungry by now, aren't you? You've had nothing to speak of since breakfast.'

His fingers rippled down her spine and smoothed the curve of her hip. 'I saw you disobeying my orders and running about the park this morning. I would have joined you, except that women seem to think it's bad luck for a man to see his bride before the wedding.'

'I'm not superstitious . . . and I hadn't promised to obey you then. I will from now on.'

She felt his silent laughter. Presently, he said, 'This time tomorrow we should be back where we started, on board *Rain*.'

'You said you had another surprise for me.'

'So I did.' He put her gently aside, and sprang off the bed. Francesca watched him move to a table and take something from the top of it. Her husband. Her lover. Her friend. She was glad now that she had waited for him. Nothing but the best—a sound rule in every sphere of life.

'Come here by the window,' he said.

She swung her slim legs to the floor and went to where he was standing, his tall figure lined with silver.

He was holding a small flat case and, when he opened it, the dazzle within made her blink. As he moved the box this way and that, she felt she was seeing a tiny piece of the moon-glade at which she had so often gazed on the nights she had spent aboard *Rain*.

And then, as he held the box still, she knew what it really was.

'Oh, Caspar . . . *a rain of diamonds*!' she exclaimed, in a whisper.

'You can't see it properly in this light.'

He moved to switch on a lamp, then gave her the case so that she could see it in detail.

She had seen many beautiful jewels in the windows of jewellers in London and Paris and Rome, but never one as lovely as this.

From a graceful flower spray, each petal and leaf encrusted with large and small diamonds, depended five separate strands of graduated stones, each strand ending in a point like a tiny icicle.

'I almost didn't have it,' said Caspar. 'A long time ago, before I decided you must have got over your calf love, I asked both Sotheby's and Christie's to let me know the next time a rain was catalogued. They warned me it might be a long wait because antique diamond jewellery is so often broken up and re-set. That one came up in a sale two months ago. I went to bid for it myself, and nearly backed out towards the end. It seemed rather futile to buy it when the only woman I would give it to had gone out of my life and was probably married to someone else.'

Francesca lifted the rain from its bed of black velvet. The stones flashed and burned with white fire. Each pendant strand, finely jointed, continued to tremble for some moments: the effect was raindrops shaken off by a breeze through the leaves.

Francesca went to the mirror and, taking the spray carefully between her fingers and thumbs, held it against her, below the hollow of her throat.

'If we have a fine chain made for it, you can wear it as a necklet as well as a brooch,' Caspar suggested.

She didn't reply. Looking over the top of her head, he saw the tears in her eyes and the tremulous movement of her lips.

Taking the jewel and putting it aside, he folded her in his arms and began to kiss her wet lashes and soft, willing mouth.

'I wanted to do that the first time you cried over a present,' he murmured, after a while. 'But you were impossibly young. It couldn't have worked.'

'Perhaps not.'

She felt sure her love for him would never have wavered. But, thinking back to the girl she had been at nineteen, she doubted if, then, she had had enough to give him.

Presently, with the rain of diamonds pinned to the cloud of apricot chiffon which went over an even more diaphanous trousseau nightdress, she and Caspar—he in the red silk dressing-gown she remembered from her first night at Lanyon—went to the Cabinet to have supper, and to talk about *Rain* and the islands.

Later still, when the great house was full of the sound of clocks striking midnight, and although on this occasion she was wearing quilted silk mules, he swept her up in his arms and carried her back to their bedroom.

Then, knowing they could sleep tomorrow while the plane carried them back to the blue Caribbean, they spent the night making love and being very happy.

THE GREAT COCO CHANEL

The world of high fashion is full of intrigue and fierce competition. It is also a world dominated by men. And yet one of the most influential figures in the history of modern fashion was a woman—Coco Chanel. So rich and colorful was her life that it was the inspiration for a hit broadway musical called—what else—*Coco!,* starring Katharine Hepburn.

Born in 1883, Gabrielle Bonheur Chanel began her career as a hatmaker in Paris in 1912. Aided by a wealthy patron, her talent and reputation grew, and soon she began to design dresses. By the mid-1920s the simple and restrained "Chanel look" had swept Europe, revolutionizing the style of women's clothing.

Chanel was the first to cast off whalebone corsets, to wear costume jewelry and to shock society by appearing in pants. Women from every walk of life rushed to imitate Chanel's eccentricities.

But Chanel was more than a trendsetter. She was an intimate friend of such great artists and musicians as Picasso and Stravinsky. And while she never married, she had many lovers, one of whom was the Duke of Westminster.

During World War II, Chanel closed her fashion house and retired. However, such an active spirit could not remain idle for long, and at the age of seventy-one Chanel reopened the House of Chanel. Within a few months her name and power reigned supreme once again.

Coco Chanel died in 1971, and the comment of one distinguished journalist might serve as an epitaph: "Chanel...helped to form my notion of elegance, of culture and of style."

4
FREE
Harlequin Romances